# BIG LOVE

## A Novella

## MICHAEL EHRET

Scrivenings
PRESS
Quench your thirst for story.
www.ScriveningsPress.com

Published by Scrivenings Press LLC
15 Lucky Lane
Morrilton, Arkansas 72110
https://ScriveningsPress.com

Printed in the United States of America



Second Edition

This novella was originally published in *Coming Home: A Tiny House Collection* by Penwrights Press on May 15, 2017. It has been republished "as is" with permission from the previous publisher and with a new added epilogue.

Paperback ISBN 978-1-64917-381-2

eBook ISBN 978-1-64917-382-9

Cover by Linda Fulkerson, www.bookmarketinggraphics.com

I was so impressed by the fresh, new voice in *Big Love*! I'm waiting anxiously for his next book.

— Ane Mulligan, author of the award-winning
Georgia Magnolias series

*Big Love* is a breath of literary fresh air with characters whose voices were so unique and likable and dialogue that made me want to spend the day with these people. I was never sure where the plot would ultimately take me, but I happily followed it through each scene and sighed with satisfaction at the conclusion, wishing the story wasn't over so soon.

— Deborah Raney, author of the Camfield
Legacy series and *A Nest of Sparrows*

The characters are believable. The settings are well-developed. The blend of tension/pain alongside hope/joy is well-executed. I really enjoyed the story.

— Jeff Crosby, author of *The Language of the Soul*

# Chapter One

I'm just going to put it out there. My name's Timberly. Yeah, Timberly. Get over it. I did long ago, okay? What can a girl say? My father, the dealmaker, cut what he called a "win-win" with my mother. Trouble is, there were three people in the deal and only two of them "won-won."

Mom knew I was a girl and wanted to call me Kimberly after her best friend in high school. Dad—Timothy Robert Charles— wanted a boy to "carry on the family name and name after me." No one really asked me, which was probably good because I dislike both the K and the T versions.

And, no, in case you're wondering, I was never confused about who I am. I decided early on who I was and who I wanted to be. Let me start over.

I'm Berly Charles. I live in Broad Ripple, with my four-legged main crush, Baxter, my mini Schnauzer. The Ripple used to be the coolest neighborhood in Indianapolis but isn't anymore, now that the people looking to gain cool by osmosis have overtaken it. But I still like it. I'm single, twenty-nine, naturally redheaded, and sassy. And I like it that way—most of the time.

Other times? Well. Why don't I tell you what I do for a living?

During the day I run a tiny construction company that's part of my dad's conglomerate, King Charles Enterprises. Yeah, I know, ego much? But I love my dad, and he did give me one thing—other than the strangest name of all my friends. He gave me tenacity. And a mind for business. So, that's two, I guess. Plus the name. Okay, three. And he did love me. We'll go with four and an option to upgrade.

When I said I run the tiny construction company you probably thought it was a little, boutique-like construction business my dad set up for me to build a house or two a year and feel like I'm doing something meaningful. It's okay. Lots of people think that. If you did, you're wrong too.

La Petite Maison, LLC—so, shoot me, I majored in French for a brief shining moment—is my construction company that builds tiny houses. Homes just like yours, at a fraction of the size (and cost). And it is mine, not King's. It's housed under the family corporation because it's better for business, but I run it.

I hold meetings at homeless shelters and under highway overpasses in the parts of town most people just drive over. Well, mostly. I do have an office and a desk at King, but I don't go into Edward's territory willingly. My real office is in my home and out at the sites.

Who is Edward? He's my baby brother by seven years. Let's just say Edward and I were raised in two different families. He doesn't get me and I stopped a couple years ago trying to understand how he can be so completely soulless.

I try to be generous. I've seen ungenerosity. Been the recipient of it. And it cuts to one's core. To me, refusing to be generous is denying the other person's humanity. How can a Christian—and I am one—look at someone in need and turn his back, roll up his window, pretend not to see? This is Edward. I love my brother, but he is a bit of a tool.

I should be honest. La Petite Maison isn't exactly rolling in dough. Don't get me wrong; I'm not about to be turned out on the street—not this time. But if things don't turn around soon, Edward, Daddy's chosen successor, will be justified in recommending to the board, as he swears he's going to, that they shutter me.

In starting the business, I asked Daddy for the freedom to build a tiny home now and then at cost—or less—for people who need a home. Edward hated the idea, but with Daddy's assistance I was able to build the vision into the margins.

Edward and I differ on the definition of "now and then." Now that Daddy's gone, I've lost my protector. I can't say Daddy liked me giving homes away, but I can say he understood why. We lived it together. Edward did not. And maybe that's the difference.

One good thing is that Edward's not an idiot. Definitely a tool, but not a fool. He'd stop the saber waving if I could show a healthier bottom line.

So, I need to hike up my big girl panties and find a way. And I may know just the woman to help.

Nathan Rafferty, or Rafe as the few he allowed close called him, strode into his office and paced in front of the window that afforded him one of the most enviable lake views in all of Chicago. How had he been roped into this? Him? Of all people?

The feature articles he wrote for *architecture journal*—oh how he hated the pretentious use of all lower-case that came about two years ago with the new hipster managing editor, Holden Fields—were about the biggest and the best architectural accomplishments of the modern world.

Petronas Towers, Kuala Lumpur.

The Bird's Nest in Beijing.

Hotel Remota, Puerto Natales, Chile.

These were the types of projects Nathan Rafferty, magna cum laude graduate of the Lyles School of Civil Engineering at Purdue University, wrote about. Real Architecture. Important, trend-setting, place-creating Architecture. Projects worthy of his attention.

Tiny houses were not. Not places even smaller than the rat holes he grew up in. Definitely in the "not worthy" category.

He stood behind his expansive two-toned wooden desk, his hands splayed over the smooth surface, claiming it, owning it. Taking dominion over things, even other people, when necessary, always brought back his sense of control. And he needed that sense reinstated. He needed it reinstated right now, baby.

As the senior writer—and should-have-been editor—he ought to get to choose his own assignments. That was the unassailable argument. Yet it had failed.

It was the twit. That twit admin. Bitsy, Betsy, Twitsy, whatever. This was her fault.

In that morning's editorial meeting, where everyone pretends that all stories are available to anybody, regardless of who they might be—but they really aren't, Twitsy's annoying little bird chirp of a voice had rung out as Hipster Holden was preparing to make assignments for an upcoming issue.

"Wouldn't it be, you know, sort of cool and all if Mr. Rafferty would, I don't know, take on the tiny home story?"

"Absolutely not," Rafe had said immediately, nipping that idea in the bud.

The admin squirmed a little, and he was glad to see his remark had the desired effect.

"But," she stammered, getting her gumption on now, "it's a hot trend right now and he's—you're—our Trends writer. Your name on it would get much more attention. I mean, as important as you are."

She was right, but why was she trying to massage his ego?

Holden coughed and bit back a laugh. "That's actually a great point, Betsy. I'm inclined to agree. I think our readers would enjoy a story on this new phenomenon. Look at the ratings HGTV is getting for those shows. What, uh, what do you think, Nathan?"

Rafe thought he'd like to smack that smug look right off Fields's face.

"I couldn't possibly. I have zero interest and even less desire to explore such a plebeian trend—no, fad. Architecture is not about fads. Architecture is about grand statements on the human condition."

With all the calculated nonchalance he could muster, Rafe laid his notepad on the table in front of him and opened his phone to "check his messages." Discussion over. Winner declared. The crowd roars in approval.

As he peered over his phone, pretending to pay no attention, Rafe saw Holden stroke the stubble he'd been nursing into a beard for six months. This he had to see. His editor's patented far-away-deep-in-thought look he thought made him seem contemplative, was now playing out on the man's increasingly mashable face.

"Truly," Fields said, a soft Calgon-take-me-away look illuminating his face, "what could be more grand of a statement on the human condition than finding home?"

Rafe simmered, seconds away from boiling over.

Twitsy raised her hand, like the new kid in the classroom she was and would forever be, and sealed the deal for Rafe.

"The, uh, contact we have is for a company in Indianapolis called La Petite Maison, run by Berly Charles," Twitsy chirped. "In addition to regular contracts, they also do some *pro bono* work with the city's homeless population. So there's that appealing side angle. The company is a subsidiary of King Charles Enterprises."

"Not. On. Your. Life." Rafe pocketed his phone and picked up his notebook as he turned toward Holden. "Not even on your less spectacular life. I will never take that assignment."

He would not, could not, promote Tim Charles.

As he headed for the door, a low chuckle rolled from Fields' throat.

"This is exactly why it's so good to be the editor," Holden said. "You see, Nathan, that's the beauty of the word 'assignment.' Because, assignments—if you understand the definition properly—aren't so much taken as they are given."

Rafe turned. "Don't threaten me, Fields."

"Oh, I'm not. I'm not threatening you, Nathan. I'm simply stating a fact. The assignment is yours."

There was none of the traditional murmuring that marks a typical editorial meeting, but the eyes of all twelve people in the conference room were on him. Except Twitsy, who looked away with what seemed like embarrassment *for him* on her face.

Oh, we'll see about that.

"One cannot give an assignment—*noun,* a specified task or amount of work—to someone over whom one holds no authority," Rafe said. "I will not do that assignment."

"You will."

"Then I quit."

Rafe stormed out of the meeting room and headed for his office to collect his stuff, and stew.

Tim. Charles.

Granted, the man was dead, and good riddance. He'd read the news six months ago in *Indianapolis Monthly* and rejoiced. But the pit of his stomach still clenched when he remembered the look on his mother's face after she learned the company she'd invested her life—and her savings—in had evaporated due to Charles's mismanagement.

Even worse was the defeat in her eyes that night as she'd sought temporary shelter for them at Haven of Hope, a shelter for the homeless in Indianapolis, only to be turned away because she had a child. Technically because there was no room in the family portion of the shelter, but Rafe knew why they'd slept on the street that night, and many other nights, under an overpass. It was because of him.

How that buffoon had ever built anything into the admitted success King Charles Enterprises was, still mystified Rafe. He'd always wanted revenge for his mother and, if he was honest, for himself.

But it wasn't to be. And neither was this job.

He shoved some books into a box and the memory back into wherever it had come from. While packing, he felt the unmistakable pretentiousness of Holden Fields behind him—hovering just outside his office door.

"Holden."

Fields entered the room. "Your kingdom just get a little smaller, Nathan? A little *tinier*, perhaps?"

He raised his eyes to bore a hole into Holden Fields's forehead and, once again, was disappointed not to have Superman's infrared, fry-them-from-the-inside-out, eyeballs.

"Don't try to goad me, Fields. It won't work. This is a momentary setback. One that you know I'll soon right." He smiled as he indicated the box on his desk. "I'm already packing."

They both knew the start-up competition, *By Design*—no lowercase frou-frou name, thank you—would snap up *architecture journal's* star attraction in a heartbeat. Rafe would be out of work no longer than it took to make the phone call.

Fields raised his hands to fend off Rafe's ire.

"It doesn't have to be this way." He sat his Armani-clad *derrière* on the corner of the desk. "We can work this out."

Rafe saw something other than the customary arrogance playing in the man's eyes. Was he afraid?

"You'll give the assignment to someone else?"

"I can't. You know that." Fields sighed. "Not after you made an issue of it and forced my hand."

They'd had this discussion before, or one like it. Rafe sat behind his desk and crossed his arms. "Money, again." Not afraid then. Desperate. Yes, desperate to keep him on staff. He could almost smell the man's sweat—except for the abundance of Sauvage assailing his nostrils.

Holden nodded. "As you know, I'm under pressure to make the magazine appeal to a wider audience. I don't like it. I don't. You likely find that hard to believe, but it's true."

Case in point: the recent addition of "My Movie Star Home" —the latest tactic to reach the younger demo. Rafe leaned back in his chair. His lip quirked up on the right. "Don't look at me like that," Holden said. "It's easy for you. You don't have to worry about the finances. You just put words together like, I don't know, like the Frank Lloyd Wright of publishing or something, creating your version of Samara with each precise article."

Fields knew about Samara?

"Oh, spare me the squint," Holden said. "I do actually know a little about architecture. You aren't the only one."

Rafe reached across his desk for the brass sextant his mother had given him five years ago when he moved to Chicago. She'd hoped then it would be a symbol to help him find his way home. "This is your chance, Nathan," she'd said. "Take it. Forget about Indianapolis."

"What are we talking about, Fields?" Rafe asked. "I'm not doing the teeny home story. I thought we settled that."

"Tiny *house*, not teeny home."

"Po-tay-to, po-tah-to." He placed the sextant in the velvet-lined box he'd pulled from his bottom drawer. Maybe Mom had been right all along. Maybe this was his chance. Not to leave the past, but to avenge it. Still, how desperate was Fields?

"Nathan, please. Reconsider. For the magazine," Holden

said, taking the sextant out of Rafe's moving box. "We—I—need you here."

Fields replaced the sextant on the desk. "Do the tiny house story, and we'll talk about an editing position. Say, Grand Poobah in Charge of Architectural Statements on the Human Condition?" Rafe chuckled and straightened the navigational tool, wiping a smudge from one dial. "Enough," he said. "I'll stay."

The surprise on Fields's face pleased him. He set the moving box on the floor in front of his skyline view, turning his back on Fields. "But, I'm staying for me, not you."

He heard the editor's sigh of relief, but ignored it, his mind racing with possibilities as he turned back to his desk.

"Which doesn't mean I'm turning down the promotion."

Fields's smile faded a bit, but he nodded.

"Besides, I'm actually starting to see the merit of Twitsy's idea. It's an opportunity. One too good to pass up."

# Chapter Two

"I can't believe it worked, Bets." I'm nearly giddy with relief—and excitement. And I don't do giddy, so you know.

"Of course it worked. With an ego like Nathan Rafferty's, there's no way it could fail." My childhood pal and adulthood confidant Betsy Carlyle sits at my dining room table in the Ripple, both legs pulled up to her chest, knees resting on the edge of the table.

She just arrived from Chicago and Baxter nearly piddled with excitement when she walked in. Truth be told, me too. Betsy is an admin for the trendy *architecture journal* magazine in Chicago. When I called her, she suggested getting one of their top writers, Nathan Rafferty, to do a story on tiny houses and La Petite Maison. And she pulled it off!

Betsy tells me this is a Very Big Deal. Mr. Rafferty is the Trends writer for the mag. Who knew?

As she finishes the tale, Bax is sleeping in the corner in his bed. His interest waxes and wanes on people things, but my head is swimming. I'm torn. I want to call Edward and go *neener neener neener,* but I also want to treasure the surprise on his disbelieving face when he finds out.

My interview is tomorrow. *Oh my word, what will I wear?* But the story is probably three months out. I think I can stretch the budget to make that work. I think I can, I think I can, I think I can. Yeah, I'm pretty sure I can, anyway.

I pick up my cup of tea, a tangy White Ayurvedic Chai from Teavana, and take a sip, then immediately grab Betsy's cup too and head for the micro. Neither cup has been touched. Gabbing mouths can't drink.

"I was so enthralled with the tale of Rafferty's machismo that I let our chai get cold."

Bets giggled, her ebony eyes still full of the hilarity of her tale. "Let me warn you. Cold is one thing you won't get around Nathan," she said, mock-fanning her face.

"Bets, are you blushing?" I put the cups in the micro and hit the preset.

"Not exactly," she said. "But let me just say how glad I am that I love Reuben and he loves me. Because as much as I don't need the Rafferty ego, that man does make my lashes bat. And, yes, I am ashamed to admit that."

I laughed, but cringed inside. How many years had it been since anyone made my lashes bat? Do I have lashes? Do they bat? Hard to say.

"He's not your type, anyway. He's too … aloof. Haughty. Whatever. You won't like him." She unfolded her legs and stood. "By the way—"

I hate the phrase "by the way." It's what people say when they want to change the topic to the thing they really want to talk about.

"—do you even have a type these days? Is there someone in your life who's breathing and has facial hair?"

Actually, Mother's sister, Maureen, has a mustache Tom Selleck would die for. And there's Baxter, whose love is unconditional—as long as I keep him in kibble. But that's not what she means.

The ding signals our chai's return to blistering, the perfect tea temperature. I set Betsy's cup down in front of her with a clunk that sends a good swallow or two on to the tabletop.

"That was accidental. I swear."

"Uh huh."

"Well, mostly."

The wench is unmoved, her hands practically molded onto her waist.

"No, since you've asked. Edward can't grow a decent beard. Though he will be touched that you inquired about him."

"Berly."

And there's the windup, as Daddy used to say. This is exactly why I told my mother I did *not* want a sister. I whistle for Bax, and he looks up from his warm bed as if to say, "Seriously?"

"You want to be loved—and you are." Bets raises her teacup and regards me over the rim. "But in order to find what you're really looking for, you have to actually look. And you have to be open to finding."

She sips her tea and her eyes go wide momentarily.

I cradle my own cup, inhale the tea's distinct Indian aroma, and look for some sign that she's burned her tongue, so I can change the topic. Nothing. But, even if it was on fire, she wouldn't let me off the hook.

Most of my girlfriends complain about hearing their mothers' voices coming out of their own mouths. That I could live with. But how, and better yet why, do my mother's lectures have to come out of my best friend's mouth? That's just not right and more than a little creepy.

"I'm not lonely." It's mostly true. I'm really not. "I have La Petite Maison and my customers. They need me and I need them. Sounds like a relationship to me."

I'm grateful Baxter, ever the sensitive male, decides I need him more than he needs warmth. His presence at my side gives my fingers something to do other than strangle Betsy. "I'm happy. Baxter and I … It's just …"

Full stop. I'm not even convincing myself.

~

Tim Charles named his daughter Timberly?

Rafe leafed through his story folder—or, in this case, his mission folder—at his hotel in Indianapolis. Tomorrow he interviewed Ms. Charles for the first time and he needed to be sharp. The plan depended on it.

But Timberly? When he could keep from laughing, he actually felt sorry for her. Her name confirmed Charles had been the egocentric moron Rafe had always assumed. What kind of father saddled his daughter—who, by the way was a beautiful woman—with a name like that?

Well, there's a distraction he couldn't afford. He flipped the first page of the *Indianapolis Business Journal* article over, turning Timberly Charles's arresting blue eyes facedown—after one last look.

Ostensibly, this interview was about the silly little tiny houses La Petite Maison built and some alleged craze sweeping the nation. But he had different plans. Timberly would be the tool for his vengeance.

Knowing what he knew about how Charles operated, he felt confident there was dirt buried somewhere. And if that dirt happened when Charles was stealing from his mother, all the better. The man's daughter may know something about those years; she would have been old enough to remember.

After all, she seemed about his age. While he was living under a highway in little more than a box, she was probably poolside, sipping iced tea in a bikini at some nondescript McMansion on the rich side of town. Maybe not poolside. Not with that fair skin and red hair.

Unless the pool was at an indoor country club …

He slammed the folder shut and stood. He needed to clear that visual. This was his chance to put the past behind him with a well-planned slam-dunk. Focus, that's what he needed. Focus and a good run.

# Chapter Three

Rafe arrived at the Starbucks—her choice; too obvious for him—on Michigan Road thirty minutes early. He wanted to be there well before Timberly, Ms. Charles, arrived. During his run last evening, a new idea had bubbled to the surface.

If she were at all as devious as her old man he might get more information through subterfuge. After all, people tend to share more with strangers they never expect to see again than they do with someone like him, an award-winning journalist.

So, he wouldn't be "Nathan Rafferty" when they met. He'd be the more affable "Rafe." And if Timberly were nervous about the interview she might want to rehearse her lines with a kind, handsome stranger. Or at least the topics of the coming interview would likely be on her mind. It was worth a try, and he'd have his phone set to record any conversation they had, just in case.

He opened his file for another review of his research and saw Timberly's portrait again. Those eyes. So deep and sparkling with playfulness. The photographer had shot her as Rosie the Riveter, only she had a hammer in her hands. It was cute. And charming.

But the eyes . . . His mother's voice echoed in his memory: "His face always seemed so trustworthy. Something about his eyes."

Must be a family trait.

Hers were eyes he'd happily get lost in, if he didn't have good reason not to. But he could be strong when he needed to. It wasn't by accident that he was still single. There'd been plenty of opportunity—and a couple near misses—after all.

Five minutes later he was still staring at her photo when the bell on the Starbucks door jingled and he looked up to see that same face, those same eyes, scanning the room expectantly. Go time. He closed the file.

It's "go time," as Daddy always said. Time to get in there, get seated, and get ready. Nathan Rafferty won't know what hit him.

But I'm not moving. This is Betsy's fault. She mentioned how attractive Mr. Rafferty is and then got in my face about seeking and being willing to find. Was there a subtext? I've always hated hide and seek. Actually, I'm pretty darn good at the hiding part. It's the seeking that gets to me.

As a child, Edward could never find me. Of course, I didn't want him to. He is seven years younger and if he found me, I'd have to play with him. But even today, while I don't avoid him exactly, neither do I seek him out.

I don't want to seek. I want to be sought. Is that asking too much? Eric sailed the ocean blue seeking Arial. Aladdin fought back from a desert imprisonment to rescue Jasmine. Heck, even Clarice went into the cold tundra searching for Rudolph. Well, that one doesn't work. But you get the idea, right?

I want the fairy tale, the big love. That's what I was sold and that's what I bought.

Maybe Bets is right. Maybe the world has changed and

maybe I need to get over my Disney-fied self. Be more Belle than Snow White. More Merida than Sleeping Beauty.

Okay, it's on. I am at that swingin' hot hipster singles joint, Starbucks, and I'm here twenty minutes early. Chin up and chest out. I'm going to run my dinglehopper through these curls, march in there and ask someone with facial hair to buy me a coffee. And if it's Nathan Rafferty, so much the better. It can only help my cause, right?

But after I do, I'm going to kill Betsy.

Rafe ambled toward the order counter with his cup for a refill, pausing just long enough to pretend to consider the over-priced coffee mugs that he was able to step into the line right in front of Timberly.

"Refill of the dark roast, please, Janna." He threw on his best Matthew McConaghy and turned around. "Oh, please excuse me, miss. I didn't notice you. Did I just budge in front of you?"

The bewildered-by-the-lack-of-male-awareness smile on Timberly's face almost made him laugh. But it was too early.

"No, you're fine. It's a short line." She brushed a curl off her face and turned to review the bags of various coffee beans.

"Nonsense. Janna, please add this young lady's coffee to my tab." He bowed his head to the Charles woman. "My apologies."

Timberly's smile shifted from bemusement to something softer. As he took his refill, he handed Janna a twenty. "Whatever hers doesn't cost, just put in the tip jar."

As he moved to return to his seat, he bowed again to Timberly. "Again, I hope you'll excuse my rudeness."

Darned if she didn't curtsy, just a bit. His smile broadened.

"I'm over there by the window, miss," he ventured. "If you'd care to join me for some light conversation?"

"I'm sorry, I can't. I'm meeting someone in a few minutes," she said. "But, thank you for the coffee, Mr. … ?"

"Stoddard. Rafe Stoddard." The last name was his mother's married name, but he didn't think it'd give anything away.

She extended her hand. "Berly Charles."

"You, uh, you don't …"

"…look burly? So I've been told." Her smile was in full shine now. "Thank you for the drink, Mr. Stoddard."

He quirked his eyebrow at her and nodded toward his table. She demurred and stepped toward the barista to order.

"Chai latte, please. Venti."

He headed for his table. After a half glance cast his way, which he caught in the corner of his eye, she added, "Make it skinny. Thanks."

And he gave himself a mental fist bump, complete with explosion. Oh, she was coming to the table. Regardless, he picked up his phone and opened a magazine. It's good to be interrupted.

When he felt her approach, he looked up from the article he was pretending to read and smiled, extending his hand to the seat across from him.

"I really am meeting someone, so I can't stay," Timberly said, as she slid into the chair.

"But …"

"But, I wanted to thank you again and…"

She inhaled softly and the set of her eyes firmed. This one has spunk. Rafe liked spunk.

"And give you this."

A business card. "La Petite Maison? If my high school French doesn't fail me, that's, like, 'The Small House.' Am I right?"

"Precisely, Mr. Stoddard. I'm in the construction business. I build tiny homes."

"Just Rafe, please." He picked up his phone, silenced it and turned on its record feature, then put it in his jacket pocket.

"Am I interrupting?" Berly pulled back. "My appointment will be—"

"No, not at all. I just refuse to let that device interrupt a charming encounter."

And a slight blush. This is going well.

"Ms. Charles—"

"Just, Berly."

"Berly then. And I must hear more about that sometime. Tiny houses? Like on the TV show? What's it called? *Tiny House Country?*"

Her smile slayed him.

"You're probably thinking of *Tiny House Nation*, on HGTV."

"Ah, yes, no doubt. Not a big HGTV watcher."

"Oh, what do you watch?"

"I have my own preferred alphabet soup network."

"Let me guess. ESPN?"

He feigned indignation and leaned forward into the conversation. Her perfume, not noticeable until he got close, reminded him of a spring rain.

"Is that all you see in front of you, Ms. Charles? A has-been jock reliving his former glories by watching younger jocks live out theirs?"

A faint pink glow spread over her—*were those freckles?*—cheeks as she stumbled in that awkward space where one is suddenly unsure if a *faux pas* has been committed.

"Well, um, of course not." The pink deepened.

Berly's fluster may have been the most charming thing he'd seen in, actually, forever.

She removed the lid from her cup and blew on her drink. "I mean, a man like you probably spends his nights, at least the nights when he's alone, which are likely few, with something like . . . the History Channel?"

His guffaw caused her to sit back in her chair. He held up his hands to ward off her concern.

"No, no. You're right. I do spend way too many nights in front of ESPN, but I was actually thinking of CN."

Berly leaned across the small table between them. "That was not funny, Mr. Stoddard." However, the twinkle in her eyes belied her statement.

"Tell me about your company. Why tiny houses?" What could possibly interest Tim Charles's daughter in a closet on wheels?

Her gaze softened, her smile—always bright—became radiant. "How best to explain it, other than I'm just fascinated by them." She looked out the window, almost as if seeing the story play out in the Starbucks parking lot. When she turned back to him, her eyes were smoky with memory.

"Once upon a time there was a princess. Her father, the King, wasn't really a great king. There was no 'on the job training' for kings at the time, so he did what he thought was best. And it often wasn't."

Rafe leaned in, captured by the story and the storyteller, yes, but also so his phone would be sure to record the conversation.

"The King, though he loved his queen and the princess dearly, one day lost his castle because he couldn't make the castle payment—again. On that day, the princess came home and found all of her ponies, scepters, and crowns boxed up and sitting on the road with no home to go to."

He watched as she looked down into her drink and he wondered what she saw there.

"That's the day I learned a little about what it was like to be homeless, Rafe. We were lucky. Daddy had many friends, and we survived to win back the kingdom eventually. My father was Tim Charles, president of King Charles Enterprises."

This was not the tale Rafe expected to hear.

"Daddy didn't always make good choices, but on that day, when he lost his business and our home, he did. We ended up staying with a family from our church until he got back on his feet. They, particularly the husband, were instrumental in helping him find his way."

She took a sip of her chai, both hands wrapped around the cup.

"I was eight. But I was old enough to realize how close we came to living on the street, but for the kindness of that family. It may sound Scarlett O'Hara-ish, but I vowed that day that I would never be homeless again—and that I would do whatever I could to help provide homes for others."

"Ah," Rafe interjected. "Enter La Petite Maison."

Berly nodded. "We provide as many homes as the bottom line allows, at cost, to people living on the streets." Her warm glow cooled a bit. "Well, we did while Daddy was alive. Now, we help as many as Edward will allow me to help."

She turned her head slightly to the right and smirked. When she did, her amber curls caught the soft light of the coffee shop and made Rafe think of an early fall picnic shared on a homemade quilt. He mentally smacked the image out of his head. He didn't even like picnics.

"Edward?" Rafe asked.

"My brother, the CEO of King Charles."

So, Edward wasn't a significant other. Good.

Rafe pointed at her hands. "Do those actually swing hammers or just push pens across paper?"

"Mr. Stoddard," she chided, "you're sexist."

He raised his hands in surrender. "No, not at all. I just have some projects, and God knows I'm no good with tools. Every time I try to hammer a nail, it either bends or I hit my fingers. I'm cursed." He crossed his arms on the table and leaned toward her. "Maybe you'd like to come over and drive a few nails for me?"

But Berly didn't take the bait. Instead, she gave him a look that indicated he'd have to try harder. He did like a challenge.

"Didn't your father teach you how to hammer," she asked. "That's how it usually happens."

Rafe clenched his teeth. "Yeah, not so much. No father."

For the second time, he saw Berly backpedal mentally and berated himself. He wanted—needed—her to feel comfortable with him.

"Well, of course I have a father. Let's just say he wasn't in the picture. And I'm not really interested in hammers, anyway."

"I'm sorry, Rafe. I didn't mean to pry." Berly reached across the table and lightly touched his hand. The warmth in her fingertips traveled straight up his arm and into his heart.

The empathy in her eyes undid him. He needed to get this discussion back on track. He wanted to learn about her father, not talk about his own pathetic excuse for one.

He cleared his throat. "So, Berly, I assume your father taught you to hammer. What else did he teach you?"

"Oh, many things." She picked her next words carefully. "Life with Daddy was always an adventure."

"And was that a good thing?"

"Adventures? Adventures are always a good thing. Without them, life gets stale like the unwanted heel of a loaf of bread. Eventually the edges curl up and the bread starts to turn green. Not attractive."

"So, if your life is getting moldy…"

". . . you need an adventure!"

He loved the way being with her made him think about life—and himself—differently. "You were talking about things your father taught you," he prompted.

"We don't have enough time for those stories," she said. "But just one quick thing I will share. Daddy taught me the importance of investing in others. He opened his business and his life to men who needed guidance."

And once again, her eyes drilled into his and he couldn't look away.

"I wish you could have known my father—when you were a child, I mean. He was always building something, often with the neighborhood boys helping. He would have taught you to hammer and more."

Had he underestimated Tim Charles or was this a doting daughter's interpretation of reality? Rafe found it hard to doubt her words. He had never met someone so sincere, yet direct. He leaned back in his chair to take her in fully.

Berly appeared to interpret that as the end of the conversation and stood to go. "I should get a table for my meeting. It was—wonderful to meet you. Thank you, Mr. Stoddard, I mean, Rafe. For the chai, as well."

Rafe stood, anxious to keep the conversation going. "No, really, you don't need to go yet." He groped for a way to keep her at the table. "Maybe *you* could teach me how to hammer?"

She laughed and pushed her card to his side of the table. "La Petite Maison is having a charity build next month. We're going to try to build five tiny houses in one day. If you're serious about learning to hammer, call me and I'll give you the details for the build."

She hesitated. "Maybe I'll teach you my hammer tricks then."

"I'll be in town again next week, Ms. Charles." He paused and dropped his gaze momentarily. He didn't want to wait until next month to see her again. He looked purposefully into her eyes. "May I call?"

He watched a response war over her face and feared she might decline. Instead she straightened her back, held his gaze, and pointed to the table. "You have my card." She picked up her chai and turned to walk away, then looked back. "I didn't give it to you as a social courtesy, Rafe."

And now he was the flummoxed one. "I, um, great. I'll be in touch."

Her face turned slightly puzzled. "Earlier, you said you

watched 'CN' when we were talking about alphabet soup networks. Did you mean CNN?"

Rafe chuckled and shook his head. This one picks up on the details; he'd have to watch himself. "No, Cartoon Network."

Berly's smile returned full force. "I'm more of a Disney girl myself, but I've been known to watch a little 'Gumball' now and then."

His surprise must have shown.

"Did you think you were the only fan of cartoons for adults?" Her gaze appraised him. "I'm betting you're a 'Steven Universe' type."

Rafe stood to follow after her to her new table. He didn't want to leave, but he couldn't figure out a reason to stay. "I DVR 'Steven Universe.'"

She nodded, as if recording a cartoon were the most natural thing to do.

"Berly, are you sure your meeting is going to happen? Isn't this guy late already?"

She cast him an odd look.

"I don't think I mentioned my appointment was with a man, Mr. Stoddard."

Clean up on Aisle 7!

"No, I guess not. That was an assumption on my part." He grimaced and ran his hands through his hair. "And so we end as we began, with me apologizing. And, I do."

Her guard lowered to half-mast. "No need. But since my best friend is the administrative assistant in Mr. Rafferty's office, I'm pretty sure he'll show up. She set the meeting."

Rafe froze. Twitsy was her best friend? The one who suggested the story?

"Mr. Stoddard? Are you all right?"

Rafe wiped the stunned look from his face and forced his smile back into place. "Yes, I'm fine. Too much caffeine, I fear." Or too much intrigue.

"Well, enjoy your meeting," he said. *The one that is never going to happen.*

"Thank you. I look forward to next week," she said.

Rafe nodded. "As do I. As do I."

He walked out the door, wondering what kind of game was being played—and who was the patsy?

*How long do I stay?*

In college, it was twenty minutes for a prof, but only ten for a teacher's assistant. Poor TAs got no respect. But, how long does a reporter get? One who is going to change your world for the better?

Rafe left twenty minutes ago, but I still smell his cologne. Not that I mind. It makes me think of Daddy, though he rarely wore cologne. Not unless Mother insisted. He always claimed he was too ugly to smell pretty.

Rafe will never be able to make that claim. Those eyes. Something about the eyes. If the eyes are the windows to the soul, I want a deeper look at Rafe's soul.

But his scent still reminds me of Daddy. His strength, his presence. I guess that's okay. Betsy channels Mom, and Rafe makes me think of Dad. At least no one makes me think of Edward. One Edward is more than enough.

Nathan Rafferty, on the other hand. I've never even met the man, but he's on my naughty list. Couldn't he at least have called? I probably missed a delightful dinner with Rafe so I could sit here, alone, in a Starbucks. No wonder no one at the magazine likes him.

And I may now never know if I would have batted my eyes at him. However, I am pretty sure I batted my eyes at Rafe. More than once. In fact, I think I have BEF, batted eye fatigue.

Who is he? What does he do? I didn't ask any questions, and

he did not give me a business card back. He said he'd be "back in town" next week, but from where? I could never be a reporter.

Not that it matters, really. He probably won't call. He was just being polite. In fact, he'll likely return to wherever he came from and thank his lucky stars that I had an appointment.

*Who are you kidding, girl?* That man is probably out in the parking lot right now planning a way to ride in on his white horse and save me from the boring, late, inconsiderate clod that is Nathan Rafferty.

Unless there's an Evil Queen. There's always an Evil Queen.

Bets is going to have some explaining to do.

Twenty minutes after he left the coffee shop, Rafe, deeply engrossed in sorting the angles and analyzing the situation, blew by the city of Lebanon on I-65 heading back to Chicago. What did Berly know and when did she know it? Had he underestimated the devious nature of the Charles family?

Her smile and those blue as the deep blue ocean eyes had penetrated him, dissolved his guard, and made him susceptible to being led astray. Was that what happened? He didn't want to believe it, but it *was* an option.

He must also allow the possibility that Berly was exactly as she appeared—beautiful, charming, independent, and, well, beautiful. Inside and out. After all, she watched "Gumball," at least sometimes. And there was her commitment to helping get the homeless off the streets.

From the moment he'd seen her in person he'd lowered his guard. Could she be underhanded enough—like him—to pretend she was someone she wasn't? Impossible.

His mother never thought Tim Charles had done what he'd done on purpose or with evil intent. In fact, she'd encouraged

Rafe to give up his anger and resentment. But he'd convinced himself that Charles had intentionally stolen his family's money.

It was Tim Charles's fault Rafe had lived in a shack under an overpass. It had to be. That's what made sense. At least, until now. Tim Charles as a loving father who built things with neighborhood boys? That didn't fit the picture.

What was Rafe to do now? What should he think?

Because he really thought, as impossible as it should be after just one meeting, he was falling for Berly Charles. What had he done, lying about who he was? And how could he fix it?

He knew at least one thing for certain. Twitsy had some explaining to do.

# Chapter Four

Bets isn't answering her phone. She goes to all of this trouble to set up an interview with the vaunted Nathan Rafferty, and he can't be bothered to show. Now, when I want to complain—and, let's face it, talk about Rafe—she is nowhere to be found.

How can this be? I leave what I hope is not a desperate-sounding "Call me!" voicemail.

I can't stop thinking about coffee with Rafe. I've told Baxter about it twice, but he just wags his stub of a tail and sits on my lap gazing at my croissant. He seems entirely unconcerned about the possible presence of another male in my life.

*Hold on there, Berly girl.* Don't jump the gun. Rafe hasn't even called and, considering it's been three whole hours since we met, he probably won't.

I need Betsy, and pretty darn quick. Before thoughts of Rafe Stoddard undo me.

The ring of my phone sends Baxter scurrying. Finally! I was beginning to fear my phone would never ring again.

"Bets, where have you been? I've been calling and texting for hours."

"Um, hello? This is Janna? From the Starbucks on Michigan Road?"

Oh great, a question talker. Grr. How can this not be Betsy? I need it to be Betsy.

"Sorry I thought you were someone else." And you should be.

"That's okay. I'm calling for an, um, Berly Charles? Is ... he there?"

Normally it amuses me to toy with people who wonder if "Berly" is male or female, but today? Not so much. Today this caller is not Bets and is therefore tying up my line unnecessarily.

"How can I help you?"

"Is this Berly?"

"Did you call my phone?"

"Um, Ms. Charles? Sorry to bother you, but we found your notebook? On one of our tables? I just wanted to let you know we have it behind the counter."

I pause, waiting for the expected question.

"If you wanted to pick it up?"

There it is! Normally, I am not speechless. But it takes me a while to respond.

"Ms. Charles?"

"Sorry. But, I didn't leave a notebook there."

"Oh. Well, we found your business card on top of the notebook? And assumed it was yours?"

Get a spine, girl. Make a statement for once in your life. But question talkers rarely do. I feel like I'm in a *Seinfeld* episode.

Okay then, no wonder Rafe hasn't called. He walked off without my card. And it's only been three hours and five minutes. But if it's not my notebook, then it must be his. I could learn something about my mystery man!

"Ms. Charles?"

I really need to focus.

"Yes, thank you. I remember now. I'll come by and pick it up right away."

"No need to hurry. We'll hold it behind the counter until it's convenient?"

Oh, it's convenient. Very convenient. No question about it.

"On my way?" I know it's mean, but I couldn't resist. I actually giggle as I hang up the phone.

With Bax as Gene Kelly and me as Debbie Reynolds, I dance around the house, my mind filling with possibilities.

Rafe pulled into the garage of his Lake View apartment building. After spending half of the three-plus hour drive from Indianapolis puzzling over whether Berly was playing him or he was playing her, he'd found himself for the last half of the drive revisiting their conversation about fathers, of all things.

That and mentally gazing into those arresting blue eyes of hers. He'd imagined his hands on the steering wheel were actually tangled in her amber hair. The bouquet of her perfume teased his memory.

He didn't remember the traffic, the turns, the tolls of his trip —he'd engaged in automatic driving at its finest—but he'd seen every detail of their table at Starbucks, heard every trill of her laugh, felt all of the heat of her touch. And it had unnerved him.

How was it, sitting in his car in the garage, he could still hear her voice?

He pulled his phone out of his pocket, found the file of their conversation, and moved the slider to just past the midpoint. He heard his own voice and thought how little it sounded like the man he thought he was. "Tell me about your company. Why tiny houses?"

As he listened to her explanation about how her brush with homelessness had ignited her interest in tiny homes, he heard again the confidence she'd gained from that experience, and the compassion she found for others facing the same problem.

He turned off the recording, thoughts of his own experience on the streets of Indianapolis playing in his head, and exited his car. How was he supposed to reconcile his growing feelings for the daughter with his entrenched animosity for the father? Why'd she have to be so enticing?

He opened the Beemer's back door to grab his mission folder and Berly's business card. He'd call her, definitely. But not tonight. Maybe tomorrow, casual. Not desperate, regardless of how he felt.

The folder wasn't on the seat. He rifled through the stuff in the back—he always tossed his work on the back seat, never very neat about it—and even pawed through what had made its way to the floor. He peered into the front seat. Nope, not on the passenger side either.

Where could it be? Despite the impossibility of it being in the trunk, he opened it to check. Empty.

Then his mind flashed back to the table in Starbucks. Clear as day he saw the folder on the table, with Berly's card on top where he'd casually placed it after she'd given it to him. He swore. He'd been so thrown by his feelings for Berly Charles that he'd walked out without his notes.

Would Starbucks pitch it? The folder had no identification in it, just his research on Berly, her father, La Petite Maison, and King Charles Enterprises. But if they used Berly's business card to call her?

He leapt into the car, turned the key, and exited the garage. As fast as he dared, he headed for the Dan Ryan Expressway—and Indianapolis. He had three hours max, probably less. He pulled out his cell phone, opened Siri, and said, "Starbucks, Michigan Road, Indianapolis, Indiana." He had to get that phone number!

I'm betting Rafe's in sports management or something. That fits the profile of an ESPN and CN junkie. Or maybe an accountant, but I kind of doubt it. Just a titch too exciting for an accountant. But I've been wrong before. Hard to believe, but true.

This highway is a parking lot! I-465 on the north side can be slow, but I can't believe it's taken me twenty minutes to get from Keystone to U.S. 31. There has to be an accident. This isn't Chicago. We have traffic, but it's not insane.

What is the point of having Blue Tooth connectivity in the car if Betsy doesn't call? Do I want to chew her out for rude Nathan or blow her hair back with tales of Rafe and eye batting?

I'm getting way ahead of myself. But at least I know it.

And even if I'm not, I'm sure I'm getting way ahead of Rafe. Single men my age don't stay that way by accident.

Oh look! We're moving another inch forward. Hoorah. I have to get to the Starbucks by nine thirty or they'll close for the night. If this traffic doesn't clear, it ain't happening. It's five after nine now.

I wonder if he's Christian. I mean, there was nothing in our conversation to indicate it—either way. But these days, people are less open about what they believe until they know you better. That's my experience, anyway. Shouldn't be that way, but there it is.

Lots of things shouldn't be the way they are. Like this traffic jam.

If he's in sports management, why was he in Indy? Maybe he reps a Pacer? Or maybe he's trying to steal a Colt? Nah, not sports management. Maybe he's a doctor. That's kind of cliché, but Mother would love it. He could be—

My phone rings. And it's Bets, finally.

"Where have you been?" I don't really care, well not much. I have things to talk about.

"Well, Miss Impatiently Waiting, some of us have lives to attend to. I was … busy."

"First off, your guy never showed. Some reporter. Probably got lost."

An opening in the left lane.

"What? He said he'd be there."

Just as I move into the lane, Sally Speed Limit pulls over in front of me riding along at fifty-seven m.p.h. In the left lane. I swear, I do declare. I don't believe in guns. I don't believe in guns. I don't believe in guns.

"He even mentioned how he prefers to interview people face-to-face. 'Even the little people,'" she mimics. "'They reveal more.'"

Her impersonation of Nathan Rafferty made him sound oh so self-important. How droll, dahling.

"He never showed, never called, never once appeared to see my batting eyes. I was so disappointed." But not really. "However, you'll never gue—"

"Berly, I'm going to have to call you back, honey. Reuben just pulled in and I, well, I need to talk to him. About something important."

That's not a happy change of tone. "Everything okay? And I can tell it's not, so don't lie."

She sniffled on the other end. "Yes, I think so. I hope so. Probably. But I do have to go."

The line went dead. She just hung up on me. I'd consider that rude, if I wasn't so worried.

It's a quarter after nine, and I'm just clearing U.S. 31, but at least it looks open up ahead. I may make it in time.

Lucky man, lucky man. Rafe was on I-65, heading south, and he was ahead of schedule by a full fifteen minutes. Traffic had been kind and his foot heavy.

But after his phone call with Carl at Starbucks, his concern lightened. They had called Berly. Bad. But Berly had not yet come to pick up the notebook. Good. They were closing in ten minutes. Bad. But they'd be open at six a.m. tomorrow, Sunday. Good. God bless the caffeine addicts of the world, including himself. He'd be there at six and Berly would never be any the wiser.

He'd already booked a room at the same Holiday Inn Express he stayed in earlier. It was just down the road from the Starbucks. There was no way Berly would be at the Starbucks at six.

Now that the notebook thing was practically settled, he ought to call Twitsy and chew her out. She'd used her personal connections to benefit a friend—granted, a beautiful friend, but still. Not illegal. But on the gray side of ethical, in his mind.

Said the man pretending to be someone he's not in order to —what? Get revenge? Get the girl? Get the story?

Yes, yes, and yes. But could he make that all happen?

He'd worry about that tomorrow. Tonight he was going to chew out Twitsy. And enjoy it. He tapped his phone to life.

"Call Carlyle."

The admin's voice picked up on the second ring.

"Hello?"

"Betsy, this is Nathan Rafferty. We have a problem."

"Hello, Nathan. What kind of problem would that be, exactly?"

Rafe didn't care for the tone in the secretary's voice. She sounded upset with him, which irked him even more.

"A serious one, Ms. Carlyle."

Twitsy sighed heavily on the other end. "You know what,

Nathan? I'm not at work. I'm at home. With my husband. It's the evening, actually, in case you aren't aware."

"Oh, I'm aware of what ti—"

"Can this wait until tomorrow? I can set it all up for you again, but not tonight."

She was brushing him off? Twitsy was brushing off Nathan Rafferty?

"Oh, you're good at set-ups all right. Setting up your friends for special treatment. Well, I won—"

"Tomorrow, Nathan. Call me tomorrow. Stay in Indy tonight, and I'll make all the arrangements for tomorrow."

His line went dead.

She was so fired. Holden would have to hire her back five times, that's how fired she was. And she would *still* be fired.

Rafe fumed. How could someone like Berly be best friends with Twitsy? Clearly, women look for different qualities in a best friend than he would. Which presumed he had a best friend. He did not, but if he did his best friend would not disrespect his boss. Or, someone who should be his boss.

As he continued heading toward Indianapolis and his notebook, the miles flew under the car's tires. Soon the rhythms of the road beat back his frustrations and his equanimity returned. Besides he could fire Twitsy all over again Monday.

As he passed Exit 175 on the highway, Lafayette/Delphi, his mind drifted to Samara, the home Frank Lloyd Wright had created in 1956 for John and Catherine Christian, employees of Purdue University. He'd visited the home often when he was on campus and frequently since then.

Samara, which was just across Northwestern Avenue and within sight of Ross Ade Stadium, one of the busiest areas of the Purdue campus, existed in a world of its own. If you didn't already know it was there, you would never know it was there.

Wright had been eighty-seven and near the end of his career when he built the 2200-square-foot home—*not* a tiny house, but also not a mansion. Rafe had first visited the site while a student at Purdue. The home's unique mesh of style and simplicity still impressed him.

Even on that first visit, he had been struck by Wright's brilliant incorporation of functional design in an affordable home. Samara was a keystone in Rafe's understanding of what comprises great Architecture.

It's function and form. And where you can, without getting in the way of either, a touch of style here and there—like Wright's flying seed motif at Samara. This is what sets an architect apart and defines his or her work.

He had a hunch the socially conscious Berly would find many ideas in Wright's Usonian design that could be adapted for a tiny house. According to Rafe's research, tiny houses combined affordability and simplicity in many of the same ways Wright had.

He'd call Berly while in Indy. After securing the notebook, of course.

# Chapter Five

Really? It's nine thirty-three, and they're closed already?

I know people are back there, cleaning up from today and prepping for tomorrow. But apparently they all have the Cone of Silence lowered over their heads since my pounding is not producing so much as a peek from the back room.

What has happened to customer service in this world?

*Answer the door and I swear I won't even berate you for question-talking.* Not much anyway. Not until after I have the notebook.

Well, crud. Now Rafe doesn't have my card, and I don't have any way of finding out more about him. Not that I haven't tried.

Google is no longer my hero. Earlier, I found no hits for Rafe Stoddard and the few Rafe's that I found at all were references to soap opera characters with smoldering eyes and stubble.

Which, interestingly, my Rafe also has.

"My Rafe." Ha. Truth be told, I'm beginning to wonder if "My Rafe" even exists. Certainly other men, when on out-of-town trips away from their wives and families, create fake personas. But I usually spot them by the crease on their ring finger. Most aren't real bright that way.

Still, Facebook, the curator of all persons human, doesn't

seem to have a Rafe Stoddard or Stottart or Stodtardt or even a Rafe Please-Dear-God-Let-Me-Find-Something-Anything-ard.

And yes, this does raise alarms. And it makes getting my hands on that notebook even more essential.

So I pound once more. I pound as a woman possessed. I pound with the power of several years of nail hammering experience. And a face—an agitated face—peeks out from the back room.

The weasel—to be fair, he seems like a perfectly competent eighteen-year-old-promoted-to-assistant-night-manager-to-make-up-for-having-to-work-nights weasel—also extends his right arm and points to his wrist. Which is, of course, universal sign language for, "See my cool Apple Watch?"

I pound again.

He comes to the door, but stands two feet back from it with his arms crossed over his chest and mouths, "We're closed."

No defecation, Sherlock. (Hey, I'm a lady!) That's precisely why I'm pounding.

"I need to talk to Janna?" Oh, great, now I'm question-talking.

He mouths the phrase again.

"I can see that. Is Janna here? She called me and I need to talk to her. She has my notebook." I do not regret the little white lie.

Weasel takes one step forward, still keeping a distance of about a foot between himself and the door. He seems afraid I'll coerce him into opening it, when in reality what I'm going to do is develop a superpower that lets me reach through glass and throttle him.

In his best Ghost of Christmas Yet to Come impersonation, Weasel lifts his skeletal hand and points a bony finger to "6 a.m." on the decal that lists their hours of service for tomorrow. Ha, service. As if.

I try once more. "Janna. I just need to ask her a question."

The finger points and having pointed, moves on. And it seems neither piety, nor wit—nor continued pounding—will lure it back.

Where is that superpower?

~

Sunday, when the sun hit his eyes, Rafe woke with a start in the hotel room. Thoughts of "Where am I?" immediately gave way to "What time is it?" and then quickly segued into "The sun does not shine at four thirty in the morning."

A quick glance at the room clock confirmed the power was out. But why had his phone alarm failed? The phone lay, dead to the world, on the nightstand in front of the clock.

So the phone alarm failed because the charger was still in the car. Brilliant, Rafe. Brilliant.

He grabbed the room phone and dialed the front desk.

"Front desk, this is Gabe. How may I serve you today?"

"What time is it, Gabe?" His growly voice indicated the need for wakeup juice.

"That would be seven twenty-eight, sir. And twenty-seven seconds."

"Thank you for that very precise answer. Can you tell me if the power outage is all over town or when it will be fixed?"

"Indianapolis is a big town, sir. But I can tell you that it's out in our general area. IPL says they'll get it turned back on as soon as possible."

Yes, that's what they always say.

"Heckuva storm, last night sir. You must have slept through it."

"Must have, Gabe. Thanks." Rafe hung up.

Since the power was out here, there was likely no power at the Starbucks either, but that wasn't a chance he was willing to take. Besides, there might be a way to get the girl, the story, and the revenge. But he had to have the notebook, or all bets were off.

After a quick shower, Rafe threw on his clothes from yesterday, picked up his dead phone, and headed out the door to grab the future. If he were a whistler, he'd whistle. Instead, he finger-gunned the cleaning lady in the hallway, then James Bond style, blew the "smoke" from the end.

Rafe gripped the wheel a little tighter than necessary as he pulled up to the Starbucks and turned into the parking space. But some of that tension would release if the notebook were still there. The plan depended on him getting the notebook. If he could do that, he could create a paper trail illustrating he'd planned his pretense all along. Yes, weak as blond coffee. But, combining the plan with his natural charm might work. It almost always had.

So, the notebook had to still be here. Surely Berly had not made it here before eight a.m.? Then he laughed. "And don't call me Shirley, Berly."

The bell tinkled as he opened the door.

"Power's out. No coffee," the barista behind the counter said, looking like he needed the coffee more than any of the few customers in the store.

"That's a shame. While I'd gladly slam down a Venti Peppermint Mocha with two extra shots right now, I'm not here for a beverage," Rafe said. "Is there a 'Carl' working?"

"That'd be me."

"I'm Nathan Rafferty. We talked last night about a notebook. Is it still here?"

"Yep. Let me get it for you, Mr. Rafferty. It's in the back."

Rafe relaxed. Things were going to be okay. Or, at least, they were going to have the opportunity to be okay.

The barista ambled out of the back room with his head down, rounded the corner of the counter, and ran smack into a display of coffee that tumbled to the ground with him. In his fall, he dropped the notebook and the loose-leaf pages of the *IBJ* article on Berly flew out.

Rafe stooped to offer him a hand up and saw Berly Charles's face staring up at him from the floor. Carl grabbed his hand and pulled at the same time Rafe reached down for the piece of paper. Both men ended up on the floor, surrounded by bags of coffee, boxes of tea bags, and cards offering free music.

"That didn't work as planned," Rafe said.

"And yet, it fits perfectly with my day so far. And with last night, for that matter," Carl said.

As they gathered themselves and rose from the floor, the barista shook his head. "It started with the crazy woman last night who showed up just after we closed, pounding on the door, all full of attitude."

Carl reached for one of the sheets of paper.

"Then, this morning, after I worked last night, I get a call from my opener saying her kid's sick and she can't come in. So that means I have to, because the day manager is on vacation. Then, after we get here we discover the pow— Hey! This looks like the crazy woman, I swear!"

He handed Rafe the cover photo of the article, which featured Berly in her Rosie the Riveter pose.

"If that's not her, 'Crazy' is her twin. You know her?"

Rafe smiled slightly. "I know of her. I'm supposed to interview her, but I don't know if that will happen now or not."

Carl raised his hands. "If you do, keep your wits about you. That's one determined lady."

The lights came on in the coffee shop seconds before they came on in Rafe's mind.

"Yes," he mused more to himself than Carl. "Yes she is. And I'll take that Peppermint Mocha now."

# Chapter Six

I shouldn't be checking my phone during the Sunday morning church service, but since I ignored the call when I felt it vibrate —I do try to engage in the services—all I can think about is who might have called. I'm in a sanctuary of more than five hundred people. There's no way I'm alone in checking my phone. That sounds like a rationalization and, yeah, it is.

Doesn't mean I'm not going to check.

312-555-8650.

Well, 312 is a Chicago area code. Is the mysterious Rafe from the Windy City? That could pose a problem. Is he a Sox man or a Cubs man? Because I cannot date a Sox man. Daddy would roll over in his grave.

Pastor Jack is talking about suffering in this world, but all I'm hearing is the preacher at Charlie Brown's church, "Wah, waah, wah wah wah wah." I just want to listen to my voicemail. Is that asking too much?

Where's a crying baby when you need one? I could offer to take it out so the mama doesn't have to miss the sermon. That would be a kindness. Right? Lessen my guilt a little.

Silence. Just my luck.

But, now that I think about it, now would be a really good time to get a jump on the bathroom. The lines are always so long and if I go now, some other woman won't have to wait so long.

That's weak. It's not near as good as a crying baby, but I'll take it. It gets me moving. In a crowd this size, one can surreptitiously slip out from the back left quadrant of the sanctuary. And so I do.

It has to be Rafe, right? Not a spam caller. Now that I think about it, Chicago does seem like a place he'd be from. Maybe Wrigleyville? Maybe he has season tickets. A girl can dream.

I carry enough guilt in my bloodline that I do actually head toward the bathroom since that was the excuse I chose. I smile, shrug my shoulders, and point to the restrooms when the hall monitor spots me.

"Hey, I'm not a hall monitor," says the hall monitor. "I just wanted to check Facebook."

I glare at the guilt-free attitude and mentally transfer some of my own to him, hoping the weight of it comes down with a crash. But he just goes back to his screen. Men.

Safely inside the stall, I open my voicemail and find the message from Chicago. That's a good sign. Most spammers don't leave messages. I hit play.

"Hi Berly, it's Rafe Stoddard. From Starbucks?"

Was that a flutter I just felt or an involuntary eye batting?

"Hey, I'm back in town sooner than I thought. Had to pick up the notebook I left at Starbucks."

Rats. But, also, yay! He's real!

"I'm going to stick around a little in hopes you'll get this and we can connect. I have a little field trip in mind, if you're available. Call or text. I'll leave around eleven or so to head back to Chicago, unless I hear from you. Don't leave me hanging, Ms. Charles."

Can one do a happy dance while sitting on a toilet? I say yes.

I check the time stamp. He sent it at three after nine this morning. That must be one important notebook. It's now eight till eleven.

I decide to text, mostly because I'm afraid I can't control my excitement.

--I'm in. Where are you?

I thought these modern conveniences were supposed to provide immediate connectivity? It's been twenty entire seconds, and he hasn't responded yet.

--I'm at 'our' Starbucks. See you as soon as you can get here.

--On my way. Twenty minutes.

We have a Starbucks!

For the second time in two days Rafe looked up from his coffee at the tinkle of the bell on the Starbuck's entry door. This time, no Berly. Instead, a chattering mob of high school kids looking like they'd just left church poured into the coffee shop. They were dressed in their finest casual clothes. Jeans properly torn and faded in just the right places.

Geneva Stoddard would have had a cow.

Of course, she'd probably give birth to a whole herd of bovines if she found out what he'd been up to lately. His jeans were intact, but his mother would consider his integrity torn. The woman did not tolerate lies, white or black.

"I don't care what you've done," she'd always said. "But if I find out you lied to me about it, your punishment will be worse. And the truth always comes out, Nathan."

The threat had not been enough to keep Rafe on the bright side of dark lies, let alone little white ones, but it did give him pause as he considered pursuing Berly Charles—and all that might mean.

If this was going to happen, he wanted it to start off on the right foot, and that meant coming clean—sort of—about who he was. He'd doctored the files in the folder, and it now appeared that, after "discovering" their tie from the past, he'd chosen to hide his identity in service to the story. At least until he could learn whether Berly knew who he was.

If she did know about their history, he could rightfully request another reporter be assigned to the story and Fields could not complain. If she did not—which he thought likely—he would explain the circumstances to her, she would be embarrassed and he could, magnanimously, tell her it was no big deal to him. People make bad business decisions all the time. They could proceed with the story, or not, as she chose.

Feeling her father's guilt, Berly would probably choose to continue with the interview as a way of making recompense. In the course of the story, perhaps as an Editor's Note sidebar, the story of Tim Charles' deception would come out and King Charles Enterprises would choose to make things right with his mother.

Then, after it was all over and done, he could call Berly, insist it was all nothing to him, and begin to woo her in earnest.

It could work. He was sure of it. If all the pieces fell into place, he'd have his story, his revenge, and the girl. But the line he needed to walk was perilously thin.

It's actually less than twenty minutes from church to the Starbucks, but I need some time to compose myself and figure out my game plan. So I'm sitting in the car in the church parking lot, butterflies engaged in a cage fight in my gut. How will I start this conversation? A lot may depend on this.

"Who are you, really, Rafe?" Tough start. Sounds harsh. If he's who he says he is then I'm accusing him of lying. Lose.

"Are you a Luddite, or what?" Condescending. It's perfectly

okay, sometimes preferable, to not have social media profiles. I mean, so I've heard. From people who have no lives. Lose.

"Have you been searching for me all your life? Are you my prince?" Smells like desperation, but this is the question I really want answered. Right? Of course, right. Probably lose. Maybe I'll ask that one on our second date.

"'Do you believe in love? Do you believe it's true?' Do you listen to 80s music stations like I do?" Lose, and he runs screaming from the crazy lady.

I am clearly going off the rails here. Time for a quick connection and check-in. I don't usually bow my head. Not out of arrogance, but just because I'm talking to a friend, right? But this time I do. Maybe it's because I've just left church; maybe it's because my car seems to have suddenly become holy ground.

"Jesus, I can't trust myself here. I don't know what I'm doing." I rest my head on the steering wheel, probably looking like I've fallen asleep. "We've had this discussion. Over and over. You know what I want. I know that you keep saying, 'Trust me, Berly. I have a plan.' You know I love you, but plans have steps and timetables. I'm not seeing that, and it's making me nervous."

I'm tempted to rush the last part. After all Rafe is waiting not even three miles away. But I tamp down my impatience and sit expectantly, waiting for my Friend to speak. Waiting for him to pat my head and assure me he has it under control.

But nothing comes. Nothing audible, at least. But he does calm my spirit and clear my mind. That will have to do.

"Okay, I've got nothing. Give me the words as I need them. Make my path straight. You always have and I believe you always will."

I lift my head and start the car. Pulling out of the parking lot, I add one more prayer. "And, Lord, please—no Evil Queen."

~

Rafe saw Berly pull into the parking lot. Honda Accord, newer model. It looked like the Touring version, so a confident V6. He rose, trashed his cup, grabbed the notebook, and headed for the door. He didn't want her and Carl coming into contact. Carl's too chatty. Though he had seemed rather intimidated by his encounter with Berly and her determination.

Still, better to not risk it.

Ah, but Berly's no-holds-barred confidence was a primary driver of his own interest. After the curly auburn hair, fair skin, blue eyes, and that laugh—the one that started in her eyes and ended in his heart.

He had to make this work.

He popped down his shades as he exited the shop. The sun was bright—plus he was feeling a little exposed.

"Nice car," he said as Berly stepped out of the vehicle and closed the door.

"Oh, you startled me!"

His laugh must have amused her, because she looked at him sideways for a moment, as if measuring him. It seemed her glance lingered briefly on the notebook. "Thanks, it's the touring model."

"V6?"

"Of course."

Rafe nodded and walked around the car, checking her tire choice, running his hand over the hood. Trying to think of how to start.

"It's not for sale," she said.

"I'm not in the market ... for a car."

Was that a step too far? Maybe, but he didn't think so.

"Some days I live in that thing, traveling from site to site," she said, choosing to ignore the line.

Rafe nodded. "I've found you can tell a lot about people by

the cars they choose to own. This one tells me you're safe, reliable. Close to staid, but not quite. Not with the six. You have your lead foot moments."

Her hands on her waist issued a challenge of their own. "And yours?"

"Black Beemer." He tilted his head to her left.

"Ah. Well, to me that screams, Ostentatious. Overrated. Overpriced." And after a brief pause, "Compensating."

Rafe fought down a laugh and forced a frown. "You didn't even look, Ms. Charles."

"Don't have to." But she turned to examine the car closer.

Rafe peered at her over his shades, popping them quickly into place again as she turned back. Caught.

She pursed her lips. Chagrined, he dipped his head, even as a smile played involuntarily, almost, across his face.

She let the embarrassment hang in the air. "Leather, I assume."

He snapped his head up, unsure he'd heard her correctly. "Pardon?"

"Your upholstery, Rafe. Is it leather?"

"Oh. No, actually, cloth. It breathes better."

She nodded, satisfied with the sensibility of his answer. "So, are we getting coffee?" She headed toward the shop door.

"We could, but I thought we might have an adventure instead."

She spun, and he saw the princess in her eyes. "Could we? I'd love that!"

He walked to the passenger side of her Honda and waited. "Are you going to unlock the doors of your chariot?"

For once, he thought her smile matched his own. "Yes. Yes I am."

She pulled the fob from her purse and the lock popped up. He opened the door and settled in the Honda, sliding the seat back for comfort. He dropped his notebook into the door's inside pocket.

Berly started the car and began backing up.

"West Lafayette, James," Rafe said affecting a horrible British aristocrat accent before returning to his normal voice. "I have something I want to show you that I think you'll like. And let's see that lead foot, shall we?"

Her laugh didn't stop her from leaving a little rubber on Michigan Road as they left Starbucks.

# Chapter Seven

"Where to, now that we're in West Lafayette?"

Rafe has been playfully sidestepping my questions about our destination—"It wouldn't be an adventure if you knew everything, would it?"—which, I admit, I find attractive. But now that we're here, I need more.

"What do you know about Usonian design?" he asks, as I head into Lafayette on State Road 25, passing right through two cemeteries. Cheery little town.

When in doubt, bluff. You can fool some of the people all of the time if you're confident enough.

"Well, Usonia was a country created by Dr. Seuss. It was one dandelion over from Whoville, as I recall. But, their architecture —Usonian, of course—couldn't have been more different."

"Is that so?" The dog nods his head and makes affirmative noises.

"Yes. Everyone knows that Whovian architecture is all arches and curves and winding staircases, right? Usonian was, um, spare, angular, predicated on what was the best *use* of a particular design because the best use would obviously be the simplest."

"Oh, obviously." Rafe taps his right index finger to his right temple. "You may be the best BSer I've ever met, but—"

I punch his arm.

"But—oh, you want to turn right on Sagamore—you're actually in the ballpark, though Seuss is not involved."

I take the right turn harder than absolutely necessary because I can and to watch him grip the armrest to keep from falling over. This earns me a raised eyebrow.

"Do tell me more, professor."

"Please take notes. There will be a quiz."

After a couple more miles and a few more turns—including a lovely pass over the Wabash River—we arrive at an understanding of Usonian design as created by the architect Frank Lloyd Wright. Wright wanted people to think differently about their living spaces. He created affordable homes that were tailor-made, practical, and functional. Rafe has an impressive amount of knowledge on this.

"Sounds like a tiny home to me," I said.

"Precisely, Dr. Watson," he said. "Turn here, please."

A few more seconds to the end of the road and we arrive. A turquoise gate announces that we are at the John and Catherine Christian Home. This means nothing to me, but I can tell Rafe is excited.

I turn onto the red-brick drive and, after cresting the hill of a steep driveway, we pull up to a home placed among the surrounding forest as if it had sprung up from the ground. I park under the carport, though that pedestrian word is entirely inadequate to describe the brick and copper structure. We both get out of the car. Another vehicle has arrived before us.

Rafe walks around the front of the car, arms spread like Vanna White. "Welcome to Samara," he says in his best PBS documentarian voice. "One of the last homes designed by renowned architect, Frank Lloyd Wright."

The garden, complete with a sculpted dragon, stretches out

on all sides. I feel wrapped in nature, as if in my cuddly fleece blanket.

He takes my hand as we walk toward the house, squeezing it a little in his anticipation. "This place is very special to me. I think you're going to love it."

"I don't see a door."

Rafe smiles. "Wright liked to obscure his entrances. It was part of his plan to integrate the interior with the exterior. Follow me."

Just then my phone chirps and a text comes in. It's from Bets. Considering her mood last time I talked to her, I want to make sure it's nothing.

"One moment. I should check this." The warmth of his hand slips from mine as I reach for my phone—and I miss it.

-- What are you doing?

Other than having the time of my life? Rafe gives me a curious look. I hold up the universal wait-a-minute finger.

-- Can't talk. I'm on an adventure with Rafe Stoddard. Can't wait to tell you more.

Then I turn off the ringer and drop the phone in my purse with a look of "that's that." I gaze into his eyes and take his hand again, giving it my own little squeeze. "I think I already do love it. Let's go."

# Chapter Eight

Rafe walks in the door as if he owns the place.

"Linda? We're here."

In the entryway, the gold carpet—I immediately think, "follow the yellow brick road" in my most Munchkin-y voice—leads to the left and right. From the left appears a tall wisp of a woman, who must be Linda. Her short, silver hair, combined with her Maggie Smith-like carriage, give her an immediate authority.

"Rafe, you're early."

He looks sideways at me. Am I seeing pride?

"Linda, this is Berly Charles. She has a bit of a lead foot."

"She can't be any worse than you," she says, and I feel a distinct kinship. "Welcome, Berly. I'm Linda Eakins, associate curator at Samara."

Rafe steps forward. "There were moments of terror involved." He places a hand protectively over his heart.

"Pay no attention to Rafe. He frightens easily."

They have an easy camaraderie, that of people who've known each other a long time and who share common interests. I wonder what the connection is.

"Oh believe me, I've given him more than one fright since we met. I even threatened to put a hammer in his hand."

"Speedy, and brave," Linda says.

Rafe tries again. "We want the regular tour, Linda. Better get started. Time's a wastin'." He flips his hand toward the right.

Linda shuts him down with a glance over the glasses she doesn't wear and shoots me the standard "We'll talk later" look women worldwide have used forever when men have tried to silence us to their benefit.

Rafe huffs a bit, but it's all an act. He can't keep the amusement from his face. Linda leads us into the living room. It takes my breath away.

Just inside the multi-level room, she tells us the story of Samara—named for the tiny winged seeds found inside pinecones. Who knew they had names? The winged seed motif Wright designed appears everywhere, from the clerestory windows that ring the main living room area, to the rug, to the dining room chairs, to—everything.

We walk down the three steps into the main living area. There's so much to look at and marvel over that I feel like Baxter on a walk in a new neighborhood. What do I sniff first?

My eyes rest on an empty, wide-mouth glass vase positioned in a place of prominence on a storage credenza next to the fireplace. "That's a lovely piece. I have just the place for it in my home."

Linda laughs. "That vase hides a secret. Let's see if, over the course of the tour, you can discover what it is."

Ah, a mystery.

Wall-sized windows fill an entire side of this amazing great room that was created before the concept of great rooms. A line of cushioned benches underneath a wall of book and display shelves extends into and around the corner of the library section of the room.

Linda talks about how the design, the integration of nature—"With a capital 'N' as Wright would say"—and the unity of the lines in the house create a feeling of peace and relaxation today's homes often don't have.

She motions to the library's distant corner. "Wright would have said that corner bench is the best seat in the house."

I move into that corner to look at the amazing display of books and other decorative pieces on the shelves.

Rafe follows me. "Don't you want to sit?"

"Oh, I couldn't." To me, this is a museum, and that means Do Not Touch. But Linda confirms Rafe's invitation.

"No, it's alright," she says. "Dr. Christian lived in the home until his death in 2015. The furniture is intended to be used."

So I do, and Rafe sits next to me. I am sitting on a piece of furniture designed by Frank Lloyd Wright.

"I'll dim the lights," Linda says. "That will help you feel the peace."

As we sit there, in the quiet and in the natural light of a sunny Hoosier afternoon, a calm does descend. My breathing evens out and my body relaxes. It's the first time I've noticed how architecture can be used to create mood—and I love it. How can this be incorporated in our work at La Petite Maison?

Rafe rests his hand protectively over mine on the seat cushion between us. It scares me to even think about it, but I am beginning to wonder about the future with Rafe. Sitting next to him, I swear I hear some pieces of my life fall into place. I try to lean into the peace and enjoy it. I don't find it often.

"What are you feeling?" he whispers in my ear, his warm breath accentuating his words.

What am I feeling? I can hardly tell him, now can I? I'm not even sure I could tell Bets, were she here. But I am feeling.

I say, *sotto voce* but not quite a whisper, "I'm feeling very lucky to be here to experience this house. It is a great adventure.

Thank you." Why do I lie about what I'm feeling? It's what I've learned to do from too many mistakes with men not named Rafe.

He nods, winks, and sits back into the bench, closing his eyes. I watch the peace waft over him for a few seconds, but look away as it begins to feel like I'm eavesdropping visually.

After the three of us have experienced the silence and calm for not nearly long enough—I think I really could live here—Rafe says to Linda, "Tell her about Wright's theory of stuff and how that translates into his designs."

She brings up the lights again and steps back into her role as docent.

"Most people don't notice that there's no garage or basement in this home. That's intentional. Wright thought basements were too dark and damp. And garages? Who actually keeps cars in garages? Most people don't use them for the intended purpose, so why have one? It just becomes a place to store more stuff you don't really need."

Because of my work with tiny houses, this is starting to sound familiar. I look over at Rafe, who is grinning. "What did Mr. Wright expect people to do with their stuff," I ask Linda.

"You'll notice there is a lot of built-in storage in the home. The entryway, for instance, contains not one closet, but three. And the hallway back to the guest bedroom we'll see later is also lined with storage. But, ultimately, Wright would say" — and here she strikes a pose of studied aloofness, apparently mimicking the man— "'if you haven't used it in a year, you should get rid of it.'"

That sure resonates with my tiny house instincts.

She explains how Wright used built-in storage in unique ways. The benches along the wall where we're sitting in the library area all have storage under them, for one example.

I stand and nudge Rafe aside. "May I?"

Linda nods, and I lift the seat we'd been sitting on and see various items the Christians had tucked away for future use. Linens, bric-a-bracs to rotate onto the bookshelves, even board games.

Normal people lived here in this peaceful paradise. This was not an example of Wright's classic Usonian home design to them. This *was* home. This is where they entertained, read books, probably danced. Where they laughed and cried, spoke of love and argued. This is where they lived.

That's when it hits me. "Where's the television? Did they have one?"

"Yes, they had three actually." Wright had told the young couple who owned no television back in 1957 that not only would they have a TV, they'd have three.

"He also told them that they would invite neighbors in to watch with them," she says. "He was right on both counts."

She picks up a remote and pushes a button. From the storage cabinet near the open-grate fireplace, a television rises from a recessed cabinet under the stunning crystal vase I'd noticed before.

Rafe leans in. "You see it now, don't you? The tiny homes you build have a lot in common with Wright's Usonian homes— simplicity and functionality, combined with style."

I nod and squeeze his hand and turn to Linda. "Does that get Cartoon Network?"

Sitting on the bench with Berly, Rafe thought the day could not have gone better. He wanted to be with her more and more, and he was pretty sure she felt the same, or soon would. So, after feigning exhaustion and waving Berly and Linda off to finish the tour together, why did he feel as though he were standing on the edge of a cliff?

But he knew why.

The conversation they didn't have on the drive up to Samara nagged at him. He'd chickened out. When he was around Berly, he became aware of who he wasn't. And that's never a comfortable place to be.

He wasn't the kind of man she deserved and certainly not the kind of man she wanted. That kind of man, if he'd been dishonest at all, would have owned up and made things right.

That kind of man would not have doctored the evidence to fit the story he wanted to tell and certainly wouldn't have entered into the relationship intending harm as a way to salve his own wounds.

Rafe was not that kind of man, but he did have principles he tried to live by, especially as a journalist. And he'd trashed those, as well.

The last couple days had made him yearn for things he didn't know he wanted. A relationship. Permanence. A foundation. She had turned his world on its capstone and his building was about to topple. He knew it. But, even knowing that, he didn't want it to end.

What would he do when she found out? How long would the good times last? If he got back to Chicago with the relationship intact, he'd have to come up with a plan to salvage this, if he could.

That's one big "if."

His mother would say, "A lie is always found out" and "You've made your bed, now lie in it." And then she'd add, "You see what I did there?" And, yes, he would see.

What would he do when Berly found out?

Oh, he knew. He'd suffer.

As Berly and Linda returned to the living room, Rafe saw the bright "this is so cool" light of a first Frank Lloyd Wright exposure sparkling in Berly's eyes. It was a feeling he remembered well, but today it soured his mood. That light would be snuffed out when she learned the truth.

"Did you see that cute little bathroom in the guest bedroom?" She bubbled with the joy of discovery the way he had with his first K'nex building system. "It's so petite. Perfect for a tiny house."

She rushed toward him to take his hands in hers as if to fully share her excitement, he needed to feel it—not just see it. "Some of our people have done many of those same space-saving tips for their bathrooms. I can't wait for you to meet them at the charity build."

In spite of his sullen mood, he found a small smile and gave her hands a squeeze. "I'm so glad you like it. Please remember that."

"How could I possibly forget? I told Linda I wanted to move in here, and she said—"

"—everyone says that," Linda and Rafe said together.

"Yes!"

Then, she realized they were having playful fun at her expense and mock-scowled at them both. "It may be old hat to you, but this is a brand new chapeau for me. I shall wear it jauntily."

Her hyped-up haughtiness finally broke Rafe's mood, and his smile returned.

"It's all good. Set that hat on cockeyed and dare someone to knock it off. Did you get photos?"

"I did! I filled my phone. I'm sure there will be some editing to do to the collection, but I wanted to remember everything."

Rafe hoped she would remember. He desperately needed her to remember the good, because she'd probably never forget the bad.

He turned to Linda. "Do you have a minute or two? Since you know so much about this home, I want to quiz you on a couple of Wright's adaptations for Samara for an article I'm, er, some research I'm doing." One more little white lie wouldn't hurt.

Berly glanced at him then, and he thought, not for the first time, that this woman had a nose for baloney. "'Article' is a little grandiose. More like a journal, or blog, that I share with other Wright aficionados."

"Sounds fascinating," Berly said. "Is it something I might be interested in? I love hearing you two talk shop."

He had to think fast. "Why don't you start editing your photos? This will just take a moment."

Once again she pulled back, but she nodded and moved into the entryway.

I've been dismissed. To the entryway. Granted, it's the entryway of a Frank Lloyd Wright house, so there's still lots to look at, but after how well the day has gone, being dismissed ticks me off. Truthfully, it would tick me off even if the day had not gone well.

Still, I have known Rafe only two days, and he's obviously known Linda much longer.

Why do I do that? Why do I make excuses for the boorish acts of the men in my life? It's annoying.

Regardless, while Rafe is talking with Linda and I'm not wanted, I check my phone. Not that I've missed it, or feel disconnected. In fact, until just moments ago, I felt more connected than I have in a long time.

More than twenty text messages and one voicemail crowd my home screen. They're all from Betsy. Panic. Who died? What's wrong between Bets and Reuben?

I should have pressed her more on the phone the other night. I am the worst friend in the world for blowing her off so I could go on an adventure. Her first text worsens my guilt.

-- What adventure? We need to talk.

Then, two minutes later.

-- Who are you with? Call me!

Several others of like nature rolled by on my screen. I know it's been a long time since I've dated, but I'm actually pretty good at taking care of myself. Regardless, I was just about to call her to calm her down when I scrolled to the next message.

-- Are you with Nathan Rafferty?

Why would she think I was with Mr. Hearthrob-to-Himself, Nathan Rafferty? Is there a "How many times has Berly batted her eyes" metric I'm unaware of?

-- I just left you a voicemail. Listen to it. If you can.

I quickly twist around toward the living room. What is going on here? I feel watched. Guilty. But I can still hear Rafe and Linda talking.

Bets's texts are giving me the heebies, so I do check my voicemail. There's only one. I turn into a corner at the end of the entryway, near one of the three closets for some privacy.

"Hey, it's me. Sorry, but I'm getting a little freaked. Yesterday I got a strange call from Nathan that I mostly ignored. It's Nathan after all. He can be unnecessarily demanding. Plus, I had other things on my mind."

I knew I should have asked! I'm a terrible, horrible, no good, very bad friend.

The message went on. "But, anyway, he said something odd to me, even for him. He accused me of setting up my friends for special treatment. But his call came in right after I talked to you and you said he never showed.

"I let it go until I got your text that you were 'on an adventure with Rafe Stoddard.' And that name niggled at me. Then, I remembered. I met Nathan's mother once at a Christmas party with her then new husband, right after Nathan started at *architecture journal*. If I remember right, her name is Geneva Stoddard. Call me!"

Before I can turn around, I feel a hand on my shoulder. I scream. And not some little schnauzer yip as if my foot had been stepped on. No, this was a full-on-Janet-Leigh-in-the-shower-scene-from-*Psycho* scream. I can't be certain there wasn't shrieking background music.

I turn to see Rafe right behind me, his eyes wide as he looks around for the danger.

"Berly, what's wrong? Was someone here? Did you see where they went?" He snugs me close to his side while he continues his visual recon.

Truthfully, my first impulse is to fall into his arms in an exaggerated Southern Belle swoon. "Oh Rafe...," is about to leave my lips when Linda reaches me and guides me to a nearby chair.

Rafe is on one knee in front of me. It's my Princess Fantasy!

But then I remember Betsy's message and—could it be? Until I know for sure, I have to regain my strong woman cred. And fast.

I hold up my hand to ward him back. "I'm fine. Really. I had just listened to an odd voicemail from ... a friend. Just as it finished, you came up behind me and I didn't hear you. That's all. I'm fine."

Rafe stood. My fantasy moment passed. "Are you sure?"

"Yes, I'm sure. Mother always said I had a strong startle reflex. I guess it's true. At least today."

He turned his back and I swear I heard him chortle.

I stand up from the chair and push past him, heading for the door. "Are you ready to go, Chuckles?" He chokes the laughter back, but keeps that darn wily smile.

I turned to Linda. "It's been a delight. Thank you. I learned so much from hearing you and Rafe talk about Mr. Wright. I just hope I can incorporate some of it."

I pause. "It was almost like listening to two architects discussing their hero."

I caught the look the two exchanged. I grab my coat from the rack. "I had no idea you knew so much about architecture. Fascinating."

How much more don't I know about you, Mr. Stoddard?

# Chapter Nine

On the way home, Rafe is chatting, laughing, joking. But there's a little edge to it. You know? Like a dinner guest who hates mushrooms telling you how much he loves your pasta sauce—with mushrooms. It's not real. It only has the veneer of reality.

Or am I just freaked about Betsy's texts and voicemail? And about my dismissal?

We're talking about this and that, nothing really, just favorite colors, bands, movies, most embarrassing moments from high school. Typical who-is-this-person-I'm-with-and-am-I-sure-he's-not-an-ax-murderer stuff.

I like him. I do. And now that scares me even more than normal.

We're about thirty minutes from the Starbucks where we left his car when his chatter stops. I keep thinking, "He knows," which is just paranoia, but seems true nonetheless.

I don't want to ask, but I know I have to.

So, I try to figure out a smooth way to shift the conversation. I open my mouth to speak so God can give me the words I prayed for a lifetime ago in the church parking lot, when it all tilts and the mood in the car darkens even further.

"What do you hate, Berly?"

Hate? What did we just step in?

"What do I hate? What an odd question."

"Not so. We've been talking a lot about what we love, our favorite this or that." He shrugs. "But, if you don't *want* to talk about it…"

I don't. Really. So I hesitate to keep from saying the words God has now put in my mind. Now you want to speak, Lord? Really? Bad timing, my friend.

"Hate's a strong word, Rafe." My eyes are focused straight ahead on the road, but I can sense him looking at me not looking at him.

His silence gives me no cushion.

"Mushrooms. I hate mushrooms in pasta sauce. And white chocolate. It's not real chocolate."

There are times, like now, when my sarcastic personality hurts me as much as it sometimes damages those I'm talking to. Since I know this, I also know I cannot deflect now.

I look at him as much as possible while keeping one eye on the road, which is, thankfully, mostly deserted. There's genuine fear in his eyes, and I know. Women's intuition is a funny-odd-not-haha thing, but it's real.

"Rafe," I don't even have to choose my words, they're just there. "If I hate anything, it's dishonesty. A lying tongue—one of the seven things the Bible tells me God hates—tears holes in lives. Patches can cover those holes, but they're still there and the fabric has been weakened."

I look back at the road and bite my lip to try to staunch the tears that are coming. I am not a crier. But I fail. And that angers me more than the deception. I never let myself care this soon after meeting someone, and this is why. A rivulet falls from my right eye. He sees it before I can wipe it away.

"Berly. I never—"

I raise my hand, cutting off his soft words. I want to go silent myself. I want to be unable to speak. But, I can't.

"Mr. Rafferty, I don't know what your game is. I'm not even sure what your name is. But I'm not playing anymore."

'Rafe?' 'Rafferty?' I should have seen it. I closed my eyes.

How I turn to look at him, I don't know. But in his eyes I see that it's the truth. Does he care? Does it matter?

"Berly—"

"We're nearly at the exit for our … for the Starbucks. Please spare me any more words or I will have to set you off along the highway."

His head drops, but he acquiesces.

It's about a mile from the exit to the Starbucks, but it seems to take weeks to get there. When we arrive, I pull into the lot but do not park. I don't even put the car in Park. I'm about thirty seconds from an Ugly Cry that will be written about in the history books. I just want to drive away while I still can.

Stupid, so stupid.

I look to my left as he opens the door and steps out of my life. From the pavement he leans back into the car and grabs his blasted notebook out of the door pocket. If only. That's as far as my protective brain will let me go. If only.

"Ms. Charles, please… May I explain?"

But I take my foot off the brake and the car moves forward slowly. The passenger door shuts with a soft thunk.

I tell myself not to look in the rearview mirror, but since when do I listen to me? So, as I drive away, I see him standing there in the lot, hands in his jeans pockets, notebook tucked under his arm, and head down. He does not look up after me. The Evil Queen wins again.

# Chapter Ten

"Bets, why do I always do this to myself?"

She looks at me—and what a sight I must be, red eyes, red nose, damp tissue clasped tight—but says nothing while I force Baxter to stay on my lap so I can cuddle him. He has to pay the price for Rafe's, I mean Nathan's, lies. Baxter loves me, but he cuddles on his schedule, not mine. He's rather catlike that way.

"When will I ever learn?" After wearing the fur off the top of Baxter's head, I've now moved on to his chest. He's squirming, but so far still captured.

Bets, over on the couch, takes a sip of her herbal tea—she opted out of our normal strong chai—and sighs. Not me, I'm marinating in chai. I have disappeared into my papasan chair, surrounded by comfort pillows and buried under fleece blankets.

"I mean, how could I not know? Rafe? Rafferty? Only a blind woman would not see." Or the intentionally delusional.

When I reach for a new Kleenex, Baxter sees his opening and takes it, darting off to hide in his crate. "See? I can't even get a dog to love me."

Bets calmly scrolls through Facebook on her phone. This is not her first rodeo with me questioning my choices in the field of men. I get it. She wants to keep up with her sane friends too. Still, her apparent disinterest in the fact that My Life Is Falling Apart is disturbing.

"When will I ever get a friend who is sympathetic and will listen to me?" I whine while she scrolls. "Maybe I need a new friend."

"Good luck with that, honey. If they ask for references, don't give my name."

Then we're both giggling, and it feels like junior high again.

"Oh, now you decide to talk to me?" I say from the bottom of my fleece palace. "After I've threatened to replace you?"

"I've found you never do listen to me until you think I'm not listening, so I was just waiting. Besides, I have sane friends I need to keep up with."

I throw one of my pillows at her, which she nimbly dodges without putting her phone down or even looking up. Bax yips as it hits his crate instead. "Sorry, buddy," I holler, though I'm told he doesn't understand English. To which I scoff.

"Am I asking for too much, Bets? Tell me the truth."

At this she puts her phone down. "What are you asking for? Is it the same thing as always?"

I cannot believe I opened the door to this discussion again. Betsy, I hear your mother calling you. "I'm sure I don't know what you mean."

"Then let me speak plainly. Are you still waiting for a guy to come riding up on a white horse? Is his armor shiny and undented? Has this guy slain dragons to get to you or fought an evil queen?"

I close my eyes and sink deeper into the chair, but she's only winding up.

"Is he 'to-die-for' gorgeous with nary a hint of the ordinary? Is he on a quest? Are his friends amusing little talking animals that crack wise at his expense only to shore him up when he needs it most?"

I peek out of Mount Fleece. "Except for the amusing animals part, would that be too much to ask for?"

Bets shakes her head. She walks over to my cave and peeks into the abyss. "You white girls have it rough," she says, with absolutely no cynicism in her voice. "Disney has messed you up royally, pun intended. We didn't even have a princess until 2009 —and she fell in love with a white guy.

"Yes, Berly, expecting every man to live up to Prince Charming is asking too much." She heads into the kitchen for another herbal tea. "And don't think I'm saying you need to lower your expectations. You do not."

"Then what are you saying?"

Water hits china as she pours another cup from the kettle. "I'm asking you to think about what is realistic," she says from the kitchen. "And do you even want to be a princess if it means being hidden away in a tower and having to lower your hair out a window to attract a man?"

She walks back into the room. Her Lemon-Ginger tea wafts to me as it steeps. I hate ginger.

"I'm going to tell you a story, since you never asked," she says, and I cannot miss the scolding in her voice.

"The other day when I was waiting for Reuben to come home, I was on edge because I'd just learned I was pregnant and I wasn't sure how he was going to take it."

I pop out of my pillows. "You're pregnant?"

"Oh, now you're interested?" She waves me back. "Hush."

I duck safely out of reach of her accusing stare. But I know she'll give me all the details as soon as the lecture is over.

"You'll remember I hung up on you to talk to Reuben."

"Yes, that was rude."

"Did I not say hush? And don't get me started on rudeness, Missy."

She's right, which just kills me to say. I unwrap all but one fleece and sit up a little straighter. I'm hoping for a spoonful of sugar to help this medicine go down.

She glowers at me and I draw an imaginary zipper across my lips.

"When I told Reuben I was pregnant, the role I wanted him to play had his eyes popping wide open with joy." Which her expressive eyes do just then.

As she continues speaking, she raises both arms—who's not a princess?—and begins waltzing around my living room. "Then he would lift me off the couch, dance a little around the room, before placing me back down, plopping my feet on two pillows, and bringing me vitamins, smoothies, and an occasional piece of dark chocolate for the next nine months—after offering to rub my feet."

"Talk about a fantasy."

I am silenced by "the glare."

"Instead, the first words out of his mouth were, 'Are you sure?' followed by 'That's not in the plan.'"

She dramatically drops her arms and pauses. She looks to me, clearly waiting for a response. I make the zipper lip gesture again.

Another glare. "What do you think happened, Berly?"

I bring my chai up slowly to my mouth, take a sip, but I'm really just stalling. "Is he still alive?"

She sits on the papasan next to me. "He is. But only because, after seeing my reaction to his words, he thought again and added, 'Not that I'm not happy.'"

"That's still not great," I say, putting my arm around her shoulders.

"No, it's not the best, but the day got better the longer he had to think about the impending baby. My point is, I'm not married to Fantasy Reuben. I'm married to plain ol' Reuben. Sometimes he's going to let me down because of who he is—and who he is not."

"And you're going to let him down." I'm trying to be helpful. I am.

"I have never let that man down."

Zip lip.

"Reuben's an accountant. He's analytical. We did have a plan for when to have our first child—and this is not that time. What he said was not unkind or untrue, it was him."

And that makes sense. My problem is different.

"Reuben's *faux pas* wasn't a lie. My relationship with Rafe, or Nathan, or whoever he really is, was all a lie."

Bets grabs my hands. "Was it? Was it *all* a lie? It may have started out with his lie, but was there a point where it became truth, however unexpected?"

I turn my face away. "How am I supposed to know? I can't get inside his mind."

At that, her laughter fills her face and overflows until her entire body is shaking from it. Her joy even coaxes Baxter out of his crate to see what he's missing. I sneak a look to see what's so funny.

"Berly, my dear one, I was not talking about Rafe."

And now she stares into my eyes, daring me to look away again. "Was there a point where you thought, 'This man may be true for my life. This man may be the one God has for me'?"

I think about the moment in the great room at Samara when it seemed I felt pieces finally fall into place. With his hand resting casually on mine and his whisper in my ear that I can still hear: "What are you feeling?" The moment when we found mutual interests around Wright's design and tiny home simplicity and utilitarianism.

Betsy must have seen it in my eyes.

"Don't you think you owe it to yourself to find out if it was, indeed, true? Not excusing the lie, not welcoming in the liar, but exploring your truth and whether Rafe is able to join you in it. Can you let him go without knowing for sure?"

# Chapter Eleven

Rafe tried to focus on proofing his pages for the next issue, but he couldn't keep his mind off Berly. He'd read a few paragraphs and find himself thinking about her and all he'd lost. He had, inexplicably, allowed her to get under his armor.

And it had only taken two days. Truthfully less. He'd been distracted from first laying eyes on her. One could argue, if one wanted to be even more moronic than one had already been, that his current malaise was at least partially her fault for being so beautiful, and not just on the outside.

Suffering? You bet. But not more than he felt he was due for the idiocy of the decisions he'd made.

In their first meeting at Starbucks, Berly had risked opening up and showing him an attractive vision of what a real relationship might look like. One where your partner was interested in you for who you were rather than where you lived or what prestigious job you held. Or worse, how good you looked in jeans and a suit coat.

He'd been a willing partner—more than willing, in most cases—in those pseudo-relationships, but now, after mere hours of exposure to it, he missed the depth hinted at with a woman like Berly. The depth, the confidence, the humor. All of it. Yes, the red hair, fair skin, and those arresting blue eyes as well. He wasn't blind after all.

His drive back to Chicago that night after she'd left him in the Starbucks parking lot—not laying down any rubber this time —had been torture. He'd relived every moment of the past two days in excruciating detail, including the moments of his most colossal failures.

Each kind look, each warm touch, each playful jab or hilarious punch line she had given, had played back in his head mocking him. They were the recordings he had not intended to record, but could now not stop replaying. At three a.m. that morning his mind had replayed the "What do you hate, Berly?" conversation.

"If I hate anything," she'd said, "it's dishonesty. A lying tongue—one of the seven things the Bible tells me God hates— tears holes in lives."

Rafe had opened Google and searched for "What does God hate?" The first result was a site called GotQuestions.org, where he learned what the other six things are: pride, murder, evil plots, those who love evil, false witnesses, and troublemakers.

This was one time in his life when being an overachiever wasn't a good thing. He had at least five of the seven, with his options open on the others. Well, not murder, but still. He'd entered another question in the site: "What does God love?"

No handy seven-item list had popped up, but he saw a link that asked "Does God love me?" He'd clicked it, read a little, then skipped to the bottom for the summation: "So the simple answer is, 'yes.' Yes, God loves you! As hard as it may be to believe, it is the truth."

He didn't know what to make of that, so he filed it away. Maybe Berly would know, if he ever got to talk to her again.

And now, exhausted from his long night, he was at work struggling to edit his pages. In a half hour, he would meet with

Twit-, Betsy Carlyle. When he'd set the meeting, it was to fire her. It would still feel good to sack her, he had to admit. But that would slam shut a door that could never be reopened.

Which might not be such a bad idea. Especially, if it could slam the door of his memory shut as well.

His phone rang. Caller ID indicated "Mom." He let it ring, intending to let his mother go straight to voicemail, as normal. But when he thought about the conversation he'd be forced to have with her when he eventually returned her call, he changed his mind. He tapped "Answer" and speakerphone.

"Mother."

"Who is this? And what are you doing answering my son's phone?"

"Hilarious, Mom." The headache pounding behind his eyes took on renewed vigor. "Can we skip some of this today? I'm not in the mood."

"Well, you have to admit, you never answer when I call."

He stood and walked over to the window that overlooked the lake. It was true—or, had been.

"Now you can never say never again, Mom."

A brief silence filled the line. "What's the matter, Nathan? You don't sound yourself *and* you answered the phone. Something's wrong. A mother can tell."

He loved his mother, but this was not a conversation he was willing to have with her. "Just a long day. A long day following a long night." That ought to get her off subject. She wouldn't want to talk about what his long night might entail.

"More like a long weekend, from what I hear. Linda called."

Great. Visiting Samara was always risky, but he could usually count on Aunt Linda's discretion. His mother must have applied pressure.

"Tell me about this, what's her name? Berly? Is that short for Kimberly? She sounds different from the others."

Sounds different. Is different. Not talking about her.

"What did you need, Mom? I'm trying to proof my pages."

"I am just concerned. Can't a mother be concerned? Linda said you weren't yourself. That you seemed happy."

Rafe was going to have to make his aunt aware of the rules again.

"Really, it was nothing. It was probably a mistake." One he'd regret for a long, long time. "She's just a ... business associate. I'm doing an article on tiny houses and Timberly has a business in Indianapolis that builds them."

Did he really say her name? Maybe he said it fast enough that his mother would assume—

"Did you say 'Timberly'?"

Great. Just unbelievably great. He was really off his feed today. He sank into his chair.

"Because I knew a Timberly once—years ago. She would have been about eight, I guess, when I knew her. Sweet girl."

Rafe could feel the tension rising on the other end of the phone. *For once, mother, for the love of all things holy, just let it go.*

"What are you up to, Nathan?" Her sharp tone made him feel like he was thirteen again and had been caught skipping school. "Timberly is Tim Charles's daughter, isn't she? I thought you let this obsession go. I thought you had turned your life around."

"Mother—"

"Don't you 'Mother' me. How many times do I have to tell you, it wasn't Tim's fault? Sometimes investments don't pay off."

Rafe tried to get his ire up at the old charges he had harbored against Tim Charles, but he could no longer find the spark. Instead, all he could see was Berly's face as she talked about her dad and how he took neighborhood boys under his wing.

"You should have known Daddy—when you were a child, I mean," Berly had said on that first day, with the light of memory shining in her eyes. And she was right. He *should* have known him.

He had wanted to hate the man, had chosen to. Because of Tim Charles, he and his mother had been homeless for weeks, regardless of whose fault it was. His ten-year-old self had needed someone to blame, someone to make The Bad Guy. So he created a Tim Charles who was all bad. One who had no redeeming qualities.

But even if Berly's memories were shrouded in the gauzy lace of her daddy/daughter recollections, Tim Charles had still done at least one astounding thing in his life. With his wife he'd created an amazing daughter. So, if Tim Charles wasn't all bad...

Rafe had to do whatever he could to win back Berly's trust, even though he had no idea what that might entail. It may not work, but even if it didn't he owed it to her and to himself to try. But if it *did* work . . . There'd be time to think about that later.

"Nathan? Are you listening to me?"

"Mother, how many times do I have to tell you? I prefer Rafe. Nathan is who I used to be. I'm not that guy anymore. I'll call you later. Don't worry."

As he hung up, someone knocked softly on his office door. Betsy peered around the jamb.

"Are we ...? I mean, do we still ...?"

Rafe's eyes hardened and his jaw set. "You're five minutes late, Twitsy. But do come in. I want to get this over with." He stood.

She took a deep breath and stepped into the room. "I want you to know, Nathan, that I don't regret it."

"Oh, but you may yet."

"La Petite Maison deserves the attention. And, so does Berly. She's an amazing woman. I may have been wrong to not disclose—okay, I was wrong to not disclose our relationship—

but you wouldn't have done it if you'd known. You're too stubborn."

"Sit," he said, indicating the chair in front of his desk. He rounded his desk and crossed his arms, his eyes never releasing Betsy's. When she was still standing by the time he came around front, he again indicated the chair.

He saw the steel in her spine and her eyes.

"I believe I'll stand, Nathan."

He used his full six-foot, two-inch height to lean down into her five-foot, one-inch personal space, getting in nearly nose-to-nose. "It's Rafe, not Nathan, Twitsy. And I need your help."

The admin stood on her tiptoes and pushed back up into his space. "It's Betsy. And you sure do."

# Chapter Twelve

At least Nathan Rafferty has a social media presence—unlike Rafe Stoddard, who's as fake news as can be. But, I've been trolling Rafferty's accounts every day for more than a week. He may as well be Rafe Stoddard for all the activity on them.

Most of his posts look like they've been put up by his admin—my best friend—who did not lose her job over her tiny-by-comparison-to-lying-about-everything indiscretion of trying to get La Petite Maison some publicity.

Every day I tell myself to let him go. And every day my self tells me to get my own life. She can't forget his warm hands, the sly humor, or the breathy whisper of, "What are you feeling?" She's also kind of stuck on the jeans, shallow chick that she is. Me? I can't forget the lies, the lies, and—oh, alright, that dang whisper.

So I'm not over him.

Funniest thing. The moment I think about the most is when he "accidentally" walked in front of me in the line at Starbucks. That was one of the sloppiest pick-ups any man has ever pulled on me, but I was so amused that he thought he was being smooth. Truthfully, that's what made me give him my card.

Where would I be today if he'd said something awful like, "I'm new in town. Could you give me directions to your apartment?" I sure wouldn't be mooning over a lost opportunity.

Is Rafe a lost opportunity or am I lucky to be free of him? I honestly don't know. Betsy says I owe it to myself to be sure I'm sure about Rafe Stoddard/Nathan Rafferty. She says God sometimes has unusual plans for us. She says I could be instrumental in helping Rafe—that's the only name I know, so I may as well use it—see his need for Jesus.

I say, "I'm not into missionary dating." She says, "Who said anything about dating?" I say, "My heart." She says, "Well, don't listen to that. It's deceitful above all things."

And so the days go by. I remain unsure. There is attraction, but… We're now at T-minus fifteen days since Samara—another thing I can't get out of my mind. I really did feel at peace there. Was it the architecture or was it Rafe? Or possibly both?

I've been able to keep fairly busy organizing this weekend's volunteer build for La Petite Maison. I have two shifts a day for two days—Saturday and Sunday. We're hoping to build five tiny homes in one weekend for homeless people in Indianapolis. Surprisingly, Edward is for it. Not that he'll come lift a hammer himself.

I'm calling the build "Tiny House/Big Love," which is kind of cute, if you think about it. But if I think about it too much, it's also kind of depressing.

I've recruited a good number of volunteers, but, of course, we could always use more. No construction experience necessary. I'd even be willing to teach someone how to hammer. I mean, if they don't know how.

Do you know how many times I've almost dialed the main number for *architecture journal*? I do. Or I have a good estimate, anyway. A minimum of five times a day since Samara, so seventy-five times.

What keeps stopping me? Fear. I dial 312-555-272…but can never bring myself to complete the number. I get to that last "4" and I close the screen. What would I say? How would we begin to bridge the gap? Who would say what to whom first? This is what scares me.

But I miss hearing his voice. I know. It's strange and a little weird. I spent less than two full days with him.

Maybe I should write him a note and ask Betsy to pass it to him? No, that seems so junior high. "I like you. Do you like me? Circle 'Y' or 'N'." Could I stand it if Rafe circled 'N'?

I did email Betsy the .pdf of the poster for "Tiny House/Big Love" and asked her to print off several and distribute them at her church and various other places like, say, the lunchroom at *architecture journal*. Chicago's not so far to come for a good cause, right?

At least the weather is supposed to be sunny. And I'll have an extra hammer in my tool belt—just in case.

"It's going well, don't you think?" I ask Betsy, as the last shift of "Tiny House/Big Love" begins on Sunday at two. "Four hours and it'll be over. It'll all be over." And I won't allow myself to ever think of Rafe again. He hasn't come. He's not coming. I'll probably never see him again and that will be a good thing. Maybe.

"Don't be melodramatic, Berly." Betsy hands a couple new volunteers the supplies they need and points them to Mac, who will be their crew chief for the shift. My crew is already hard at work, as is most of Mac's except the new people.

"I'm sure I don't know what you mean."

"Mm-hmm."

Fortunately, Anna, the seven-year-old daughter of a friend

from church, comes up behind me to ask a question. I turn my back on Bets and stoop down to Anna's level.

"Miss Berly, why are we building playhouses? I have a pink playhouse in my backyard."

"Anna, that's a really good question. Let me ask you one. Do you sleep in your playhouse?"

"No, Daddy won't let me. Because it's outside."

"There are some people who sleep outside all the time, even when it gets cold."

"Eww." Her little nose crinkles with the absurdity of sleeping outside.

"That's why we're building these tiny houses. They're not really playhouses, like yours, these are real houses that will help real people sleep inside, like you do."

As I'm hugging her goodbye and thanking her for coming along to help her parents, Betsy hollers over to Reuben. "Finally! Our friends from Chicago are here."

Immediately I can't breathe and my heart slams into my throat. If I wasn't melodramatic before, I am now. I jump to my feet and rush to Betsy's side.

"Where? Where is he?"

She gets a triumphant look on her face and points across the parking lot.

"*They* are right there. Getting out of the green Subaru. Two couples from our small group at church."

She stares me down, hands on her I swear already widening hips.

"Fine," I say, "Whatever. I'm still hung up a little, but it's passing."

"Yeah, like someone who's had too many chili beans is passing—gas."

I smack her shoulder. "You are so coarse."

"No," she says, "I just tell it like it is."

I turn around to return to my crew, but she calls after me.

90

"Berly."

I turn back, exhaling in frustration.

"Trust God."

I nod. I do trust him. I honestly do. But that doesn't mean I don't sometimes live in anticipation of answered prayer.

But Bets is right. I need to let go and let God, even though I hate how trite that sounds. Sometimes Christianity is trite, because sometimes truth is simple. We are the ones who try to make it difficult.

My crew is well trained. I handpicked them. So I just pick up and join in with the framing. It's good to work with your hands. To use the strengths, skills, and talents you have. There's an easy camaraderie in a construction crew. Small encouragements. Gentle guidance. The friendly give-and-take of people you know well engaged in a shared task.

Focus is a gift from God. When you let the work take you away, it's even better than hot chai. Cares and worries slip off your shoulders and the world around you fades.

So, when Anna says, "Look! A horse!" it doesn't really register. Seven-year-olds have healthy imaginations, after all.

"Forsooth!"

The voice bellows behind me.

"Verily, I am seeking a damsel in distress what I can rescue."

It couldn't be.

"And mead. I'd love some mead."

I turn around slowly. Behind the mounted knight—yes, he's on a white horse—Bets is nearly doubled over in convulsions, she's laughing so hard, and Reuben has whipped out his phone and is recording.

The knight, seemingly canned in a suit of armor, headgear and all, is perched precariously askew in the saddle. This is not a man who has ever ridden a horse. At any moment he could slip and end up a pile of little more than soup cans on the ground.

I put on my best steely-eyed gaze. "What is a Knight of the Order of Prevaricators doing here on a Sunday afternoon?"

"I am on a Quest, madam."

"Is that so?"

He lifts his facemask to wink at me, as if I didn't know who it was.

"Yea, verily. Art you, um, thou in distress, m'lady? Dost thou need rescuing?"

I venture a look around at my crew, all of whom are enjoying the show. But they aren't the only ones around. The other crews are gathering as well. Oh swell.

"No. No, not really. No distress here."

Now Rafe turns to look at Betsy, who just shrugs as if to say, "You're on your own." I see there has been collusion behind my back.

He removes the headgear. "C'mon Berly, it's me. Rafe."

"Are you breaking character already?" I start to circle around the horse. It's a fine looking horse, for a rental.

He sighs and slams the headgear back on. "Ow! Nay, verily, I am a knight. I am seeking good deeds and restoration."

In spite of myself, I laugh. "You sound a little put out, good knight."

"Can I get off the horse now?"

"Actually, I'm more interested in how you got *on* the horse, city boy."

"It took a winch, wench."

And now the crowd is laughing and I am fighting to not lose it myself.

"You may dismount, Nathan."

"My friends call me Rafe."

"Don't push it, Mr. Rafferty."

He labors to swing one leg over the horse and hop off, but either way he tries to go there are challenges. Reuben comes to his rescue.

"Need a hand, Mr. Rafferty?"

"Forsooth, I mean, yeah, thanks."

Reuben reaches up to steady him so he can hoist his right leg over the horse's head. But he hoists too hard and, as his armor-clad leg clears the beast's head, he ends up sliding uncontrolled off the horse, into Reuben's arms and they both fall to the ground, where Rafe lands indelicately on top of Reuben. He rolls immediately to the right to clear Reuben, but ends up on his back wriggling like an overturned turtle.

Now the entire crew of "Tiny House/Big Love" is in stitches as Rafe works his way onto his stomach and eventually rises up to his knees.

Before I know what's happening, Rafe's on one knee and he's turned toward me.

I gasp. "Don't you dare!"

But he plows on with his prepared speech.

"Berly, I've been foolish. I've behaved very badly. I let the past and my own selfishness blind me. I would give anything to get a 'do-over' here, but that's not possible. I'm sorry, for it all, but mostly for breaking your trust."

He stands and some ladies in the crowd groan, because they were ready for the fairytale proposal.

"So, instead of a 'do-over,' I'm asking for a 'do-it-again.' Will you give me a second chance to be your friend and get to know you better? That's all I have the right to ask for—at this point."

And now the disappointed ladies sigh deeply satisfied sighs. Other than a proposal, there's nothing we ladies like more than an admission of wrong and a sincere, heartfelt apology.

"Can we try this again? What can I do, what can I say, to earn another chance?"

He tries to cross his metal-clad arms in front of him, but gives up, drops them to his sides, and looks down, awaiting my word.

He looks so adorable that I almost change my mind. Instead,

I raise myself up to my full height and place both hands on my waist. Bets looks at me in disbelief and opens her mouth to speak, but I silence her with an imperious raised hand. She'll forgive me later.

Rafe peeks at me from beneath his brow and the uncertainty in his eyes is beautiful to me.

I look at him down my nose and I say in my shrill voice, "Bring … me … a shrubbery!"

For a moment the crew is silent, then Bets says, "Really? *Monty Python and the Holy Grail*? That's what comes to you? What about 'As you wish,' from *The Princess Bride*?"

But I look at Rafe and he's smiling. He gets me. He walks over to me, takes my hands in his, and leans in to whisper in my ear, "Ni!" And instead of recoiling in horror as the Python-ites did in *Holy Grail*, it feels like home.

With that one word, the Evil Queen is vanquished.

# Epilogue

Three Months Later

I have an issue with Disney. Okay, maybe two. Possibly, three.

My main issue is their movies always end with a Happily Ever After *right after* the Evil Queen fails in her final bid to destroy love, right?

With the EQ vanquished, both characters walk, or sail, or ride off into the sunset and the guaranteed HEA, holding hands, heads held high, and music swelling.

But they don't show you the next scene! It's like their lives end there and you're left to assume they went on like that for the next fifty-plus years.

Here's a secret. That gorgeous sunset ends after the credits have rolled, and then—The Next Day dawns.

Oh, you may have two or three good months where the birds circle your head in orchestrated ballets of song and little mice squeak and you can understand their words, but then you and your Prince, oh, I don't know, have a misunderstanding? Don't see eye-to-eye? Fight?

Before long, the swelling exit music turns discordant or

stops altogether and you're looking over your shoulder for the Evil Queen again, in all her haughty inevitability. And just like that, your Prince Charming turns into Prince Sort-of-Still-OK-But-Did-I-Make-A-Mistake?

Yesterday, I suggested to Rafe we think about living in a tiny house. I think I inadvertently threatened his masculinity or something.

But what's so bad about living in a tiny house? You tell me. Wait, I'll tell you. Nothing! Not one thing. After all, that's what *La Petite Maison,* makes and sells—tiny versions of the American Dream.

Maybe that's not enough for Mr. Lake-Shore-Drive-High-Rise-Apartment-Architect-Wanna-Be, Nathan "Rafe" Rafferty.

Maybe I'm not enough, either.

∾

*Yesterday*

"Berly, when we move to Chicago, will you bring your tiny home business north or just give it up?"

This came out of Darling Rafe's mouth right in the middle of a great session of Netflix and Fill last Saturday (we're not married yet, we don't Netflix and Chill). We were binging the fourth season of *Heartland* and I made to-die-for bean dip and had been filling my mouth with it all night long.

I tend to jump to my usually accurate assumptions. However, since Rafe swept me off my feet with that White Knight escapade, I've been trying to curb that impulse. So, I tiptoed into my assumptions instead.

"It's tiny *house,* dear. That's the term the industry uses."

"Po-tay-toe, po-tah-toe."

I don't know what you do when someone who doesn't know

something tries to sound like they do. But me? I go on the attack.

"I've always loved Frank Lloyd Wright's Grassy Lawn Style of Architecture."

I could practically hear his jaw set, and I definitely felt a chill when he moved his arm from around my shoulders and paused the TV.

"Wright designed *Prairie* style homes, Berly. You know that."

I slid onto my own sofa cushion and crossed my arms. What was a prairie but a big grassy lawn? "Po-tay-toe, po-tah-toe."

What followed was a five-minute harangue from the "once charming" now "still sort of okay" Rafe on the importance of referencing the right terms when talking architecture that, truth be told, I was too mad to listen to. On his feet and pacing, he lectured me for belittling his field without the slightest recognition that he'd just done the same thing to mine.

And it was mansplaining. I'm as proficient in these discussions as he, having been raised by a daddy who started one of the largest housing development corporations in the states, if not the world. After all, King Charles Enterprises almost lives up to its name.

But mostly it was his assumptions.

That I would move the business north or "give it up," as if it were just a plaything that means nothing compared to his life in Windy Town. I couldn't possibly be serious about it. That was the message I received.

Daddy always had a saying about what happens to "u" and "me" when one of us assumes something, but I'm too much of a lady to spell it out, as Daddy did.

"Who says we're moving to Chicago?"

As the pitch of my voice rose, Baxter hopped down from the couch where he'd been sitting on my other side—paw on my leg, "claiming" me—to claim his bed on the other side of the room.

"What? Well, of course we will. I have a great apartment on the Lake and am about to become an editor at *architecture journal*. Why wouldn't we live there?"

Truthfully, I love Chicago, but I also love Indianapolis, where I live now. Mostly, though, I hate assumptions. Particularly when he hasn't even officially asked me to marry him.

Of course, his apartment is gorgeous—and that view! But Indy has great selling points too, though my place in SoBro is not one of them.

Still, if we move forward together, shouldn't we jointly decide these things? I am a modern woman. Making joint life decisions is a modern idea.

"I was planning on us living here," I said, meaning Indy.

Rafe did a quick assessment of the room. "I can't live here."

He meant my house. It isn't much more than a glorified box, I admit.

"No, silly, not in this house. Here. In Indy."

He looked dubious, but not closed to the idea.

"Well, I might be able to work remotely. We can talk about it, I gue—"

"In a tiny house."

His mouth actually fell open. Like in a *Looney Tunes* cartoon. Which was so cute. He moved a couple notches up from "sort of still okay." Until he closed that handsome mouth and then opened it again to speak. Free fall.

"You can't be serious."

But I sort of was.

"Berly, I'm not one of your projects. I'm not disadvantaged or on the edge of homelessness. I have stuff and I love my stuff."

He stuck his chest out and got to the point.

"I can afford to provide for myself." He stepped toward me in "protective male stance" which he assumed—there it is again—was comforting. "And for my wife and family."

Family.

Yikes. Another thing we haven't talked about.

This is the second thing I have against Disney. Their lovebirds don't know each other long enough to build a relationship on anything other than looks and nonsensical hijinks with animals—and the adrenaline that comes from defeating the Evil Queen.

What happens when Eric wakes up next to Ariel and she hasn't used her dinglehopper yet on those gorgeous locks? Or suppose Jasmine wants to go on a nighttime cruise with her girlfriends on the flying carpet instead of staying home with Aladdin?

Had I let myself get swept away by Rafe's rented knight's armor and fumbling chivalry? Possibly.

I stepped into *his* space. "You may not have noticed, Rafe, but I am capable of providing for myself—and Baxter."

At his name, Bax looked up as if to say, "Don't bring me into this," then curled up with his back to us.

"Further, it may interest you to know that tiny houses aren't just for the 'disadvantaged.' People who are concerned with using fewer resources and leaving less of a mark on the world we're all charged with conserving, are also taking on the challenge to live smaller, jettisoning quantities of 'stuff' in favor of quality."

I was rolling now and wouldn't have been able to stop even if I had been smarter.

"Furthermore, maybe I don't want a family."

I do, but, again, he hadn't asked.

"Maybe I'm not looking for someone to take care of me and my imaginary children."

I stood, unassailable.

Rafe sighed. Looked down. Turned to the side and took a step toward the kitchen. More dip, or an excuse to gather his thoughts?

What is it with men? Insisting on thinking first before speaking. If I did that, I'd never get anything said.

"Berly," he said, still facing the kitchen.

"Rafe," I said. The Evil Queen behind my eyes rose imperiously.

When he turned around, his face looked kind, but his words cut deep.

"You're making an issue where there is no issue," he said, softly, completely disregarding my concerns. "It was a simple question. Maybe I didn't word it judiciously, but I think you're overreacting."

At this point, my red hair was probably on fire. At least the heat rising to my hairline indicated that.

"Go on," I said, which, of course, means, "Don't you dare utter another word."

Rafe's not a dumb man. He's been around enough women to sense when he's stepped in it. He backpedals.

"I'm just saying Chicago would be—in my opinion—the easier place for us to start our life together."

He stumbled, realizing from my suspicious look that he was on the wrong path.

"I mean, there are certainly, you know, impoverished, homeless people in Chicago who could make good use of the quality tiny homes La Petite Maison builds."

He risks a glance my way to gauge whether he's said enough to not have to say anymore.

"Again, it's tiny *house*, not tiny *home*. Because, Rafe, a home can be any size or no size. Home can even be a state of mind."

I pause to give him a chance to refute my logic. But he doesn't.

He raised his hand tentatively whether to make another point or to ward off my anger, I'm not sure. Regardless, I charge forward. "Are you finished? Because I think we might be."

Rafe stopped, looked at me, confusion and hurt warring on

his face. Then he stuck his hands in his pants pockets and looked at the floor, where Bax sat, providing male moral support.

His voice was so soft, I had to actually pay attention.

"Done with this discussion, or—"

"Done."

Even though I heard the Evil Queen laugh, I ignored the witch.

Moving back toward the couch, where just moments ago we cuddled around a bowl of bean dip feeding each other chips, he stooped, picked up his Nikes, and walked to the front door.

He stopped, half turning.

"Berly, could we...?"

Noting the look on my face—frigid—but not seeing the terror I held inside that he might actually leave, he turned, chuffed Bax under the chin, and walked out sock-footed.

I heard his car door close softly and watched him drive away, toward Chicago, through the window in my door.

If he'd wanted to salvage things, he'd have stayed long enough to put on his shoes, right? So, he must have agreed.

We were ... finished.

That's my third complaint with Disney. Even when couples fight, there's always a hint in the dialogue that leaves a path open back to love. If you're smart, and you think about it, you can see how they're going to work it out.

But that's a movie. That doesn't happen in real life, I guess.

"Are you crazy?"

Best friends are always so sensitive to the trouble we get ourselves into

The good thing is, Bets knows me well. That's also the bad thing. Fortunately, we already had a Girls Weekend scheduled, so when I arrived in Chicago a week after the blow up with Rafe, Bax in tow, I was ready for some coddling.

I wasn't expecting cooing, hand-holding, and back-patting, but I wouldn't have turned down an, "Oh, poor baby!" Especially since I'd already exposed the gory details through an extensive text exchange. Now, with tea firmly in hand, we'd just finished reviewing the salient parts face-to-face.

But no.

"You are wrong, and you need to apologize."

I gawp at her. "That seems harsh."

She looks at me as if I am an alien.

"What's harsh about needing to apologize? It's biblical."

"Not that. The part where you said I was wrong."

With an eyeroll for the ages, Bets gets up to heat her tea. Baxter brings his favorite toy, an orange ball he's obsessed with, and lays it at my feet. I ignore him. So, he stands on his haunches and pats at me with his front paws.

"Not now, Bax!"

He can be so needy. He lowers his head and slinks off. I suppose that's my fault too?

While the microwave counts down to zero, I rehearse my innocence.

I made divine bean dip. Rafe ate it.

I cuddled into his arms. He removed his arm from around my shoulder.

I issued entirely reasonable and well-thought-out responses to his questions. He mansplained and made assumptions.

"The problem is you're afraid," Bets rejoins me at her kitchen table and shows her true colors.

"The prince you've waited all your life for comes along and you can't trust that he's real. You fear he's going to leave, so you create situations that all but guarantee that outcome."

One unordered takeout of psychoanalysis delivered hot and now.

I rise to my full height of five-foot-two-inches of indignation.

"He said 'tiny home' instead of 'tiny house'—twice!—when everyone knows which is correct." I am as right as right can be and clearly hold the moral high ground. "Plus, who wants to live in Chicago?"

Bets pops an eyebrow.

So, I forget where I am now and then. Sue me.

"Who wants to live in Chicago on Lake Shore Drive, I mean." I slide that in hoping she'll ignore my rudeness. Which she does, sort of.

"You do."

I look out her dining nook window and take a sudden interest in the rows of brick townhomes here in Wrigleyville.

"Whatever do you mean?"

"Berly, just last summer when you visited, right before we got the idea to try and coerce Nathan to write an article on tiny *houses*. We were shopping the Magnificent Mile and Navy Pier and you said—"

"I remember," I huff. "I said, 'I could so live there someday.'"

"Right. And where were we?"

"On the Centennial Wheel."

She gives me the universal hand signal for "go on."

I glare at Benedict Bets and mumble my answer.

"What? I didn't quite hear that."

"Looking at condos on Lake Shore Drive," I say through gritted teeth.

"Mm-hmm."

I slump into my chair, my suddenly cold hands clutching my mug seeking a bit of heat from its surface and finding none.

Then Baxter ambles over with his ball and nudges my leg again. I reach to scritch behind his left ear, his favorite place. He leans into it.

Dogs are that way. No matter how you treat them, they always give you another chance. They just want to be with you.

Sometimes that means putting up with your attitudes and moods. Sometimes, it just means giving you space.

I toss his ball, and he bounds off, only to rush back with the ball in his mouth. He sets it before me, and we do it again, and again, and again. He'll only keep this up for an hour or two unless I tire first, which is likely.

Bets is watching. She's seen this before. It's Baxter's thing. She's really watching me. Like I said, she knows me, and she knows how I think. I may be throwing the ball, but I'm also tossing our conversation around in my head.

Rafe has played ball with Bax many times. They get on famously. They both love me, so why wouldn't they?

What I've done hits me in full.

Rafe does love me. He's shown it in so many ways—huge and tiny—since that weekend at the "Tiny House/Big Love" build.

Bets was right. I was wrong.

Rafe's one of my kind, as Michael Hutchence would sing.

I've got to let him know.

Rafe walked out of his condo, took the elevator down ten floors to ground level, and headed for the access door that led to Lake Shore Drive and the short nine-minute walk to Ohio Street Beach. It had been one week since Berly cut short their weekend together, and he'd returned to Chicago and home.

Only home didn't feel so welcoming. Getting out of the condo felt good, real good, even though it was October, and the winds were blowing over the lake.

Halfway to the beach, he realized he was still schlepping about in his tattered sweats, sandals, and Cubs ball cap. Well, why not? He didn't want to meet anyone and if he did, he didn't want to be given a second thought.

On the fringes of the beach, a bench afforded a breathtaking view of the Chicago skyline and Lake Michigan. He'd warmed that bench many times when he needed to reset his thinking. And he needed that today.

The business with Berly had moved quickly—something else unusual for him. From plotting revenge to thoughts of marriage and a family in, what? Less than six months? No wonder she'd been afraid. In his right mind, he'd have been afraid too.

However, every moment he'd spent with her had felt like his true home. Her open and giving heart nicely counterpointing his closed and reticent one. He'd done foolish things and audacious things since meeting her, like renting a horse and a suit of armor.

Truthfully, those ideas had come from Betsy. But he'd agreed heartily and participated fully. And it worked!

The light that sparkled in Berly's eyes that day had set his soul on fire. He needed something like that now because he had no intention of giving up those eyes.

As he approached the bench, he passed a small crowd of people fifty feet or so to his right. They all, about twenty of them, gathered around a dog, tossing a ball. Laughter and cheering filled the air. Rafe squinted through the bodies. A miniature schnauzer reigned as the star of the show.

Yet another reason he had to fix this thing with Berly. He didn't think he could demand visitation rights for a dog he'd only known a few months, but he and Bax were best buds. He'd even verified with his condo association president that Baxter would be welcomed in the building.

But it would be pointless if he didn't find a way to fix this.

Rafe sat on the bench, determined to work out a plan to right any wrongs he'd created with Berly, even if the fault was, at least, partially hers. For a change, he was less interested in being right and more concerned about making things right.

Something sailed over his head and landed in the sand in front of him. A dog's ball. An orange one.

Miniature schnauzer. Orange ball.

Could it be—

Nah, hundreds of both could be found in the Metro area alone.

He picked up the ball and turned to toss it back to the crowd. But sitting at his feet was the schnauzer, eyes dancing and barking like a mad dog.

"Baxter?" Rafe reached a finger toward him.

The dog wriggled, its little stub of a tail driving it like a piston drives a car.

Rafe knelt and the dog—it was Baxter, he was sure of it—leapt into his arms. Rafe looked toward the crowd, but he sure didn't see Berly's flaming red hair. That would be hard to miss.

As he petted Baxter and scratched his neck under his collar, he found a slip of paper caught on the collar. No, paper clipped to the collar. He removed it, opened it, and read:

"Home is a state of mind. Size doesn't matter."

It was signed with a simple "B."

Rafe chuckled, picked up Baxter and his ball, and headed to the crowd.

He'll come.

He'll come. I'm sure of it. Even if it's just to make sure Baxter gets back safely. But being sure of it and facing that direction to see him coming—that's two different things.

I left Betsy's home with Baxter in tow. My plan was to present myself at the receiving desk of Rafe's condo and hope to not be turned away cold. Not much of a plan, but I figured the cuteness that is Baxter would get me a long way. It usually does.

But driving down Lake Shore Drive, nerves took over and I

exited at Grand Avenue and headed toward Navy Pier. Rafe had taken me to a beach there once, and it was a great memory. Maybe the water, wind, and sun will bring clarity.

I'm sitting there with Baxter, who's the main attraction, of course. Everyone wants to play with him. That's good because it gives me time to think.

Boy, did I think.

I thought about our first meeting at Starbucks and the way talking with Rafe had seemed so right and natural. I remember thinking then, *I could get used to this.*

I thought about Samara, the Frank Lloyd Wright House in West Lafayette. Sitting in that living room with Rafe everything had seemed calm and possible, well, before that all blew up and my hopes and dreams were crushed.

I was not afraid that day, but Betsy is right. I am afraid now. Not of life with Rafe, but of life without him. When I left him in the Starbucks parking lot after the disaster of Samara, I was sure I'd never see him again. I felt empty. I don't want that again.

So, when Rafe approached the beach, which I certainly did not expect, I nearly panicked. But then a plan crystallized, and it all seemed inevitable. That's the fierce romantic in me.

Without much thought, I wrote the note, attached it to Baxter's collar, and threw the ball toward Rafe with all my strength—and heart. I knew Bax would retrieve it, but not how Rafe would respond.

As soon as the ball left my hand, fear returned. I immediately turned around and plopped onto the blanket I'd brought from the car.

Mercifully, with Bax on his errand of love, the crowd around us dispersed.

So, when I heard Rafe approach behind me, I freaked. What to say? What to do? I had no idea. I determined to take my cue from him.

From behind me, Bax pranced to sit in front of me. He had a

bow tied on his head. Was it fashioned out of … a shoestring? Something was tied to it. It looked like a pop can tab.

Pretending I was talking only to Baxter, I said, "There you are, you little scamp. What are you wearing, sir, and where's your ball?"

From above, his orange ball plopped onto the sand in front of my feet.

I giggled just a little. I swear, I couldn't help it.

Bax's tail is wagging a mile a minute and his eyes are focused above and behind me.

I hear a low throat clearing, followed by a chuckle to match my giggle.

I turned my head to look, as if I didn't know who was there.

In ratty clothes I never would have thought he'd own, but looking like Matthew McConaughey with a shirt on, stood my Rafe, three-day beard and bed hair. My real prince.

"Berly," he said, extending his right hand to offer me an assist up.

"Rafe," I said taking his hand and rising.

His eyes shone. They looked damp. Which, of course, brought water to my eyes.

"I'm—" he started.

"No, I'm—" I interrupted.

"Sorry," we finished together.

Together.

Oh, the relief.

Still holding my hand—his other hand is oddly clutching his waistband—he leaned in, I leaned up, and we kissed. Does a girl get a second chance at the Disney ending?

Bax is dancing a solo Fandango around our feet, which makes Rafe clear his throat and get serious.

"Miss Charles," he began, smoothing his tousled hair with one hand. "My second presented you with a token, to which you have yet to respond. I must know your intentions before we go any further."

"Your ... second?" Then I realized he meant Baxter.

I looked at Bax and his bright eyes and that ridiculous shoelace bow and I saw the pop top tab shining like a diamond. Baxter stood on his hind legs and placed his front paws against my thigh.

I undid the bow and removed the tab.

"It's a substitute," Rafe said. "There wasn't time. You can pick out the real one at Marshall Pierce tomorrow."

His words caught in his throat, and his eyes are no longer damp, they are positively flooded with tears, which I reach up to brush away as he reaches down to brush mine.

"It's beautiful. Everything I ever dreamed of."

Rafe is still holding my hand in his right hand and the waistband of his sweats in the other.

"So, Berly, what's your answer? Will you be my wife?"

"Yes, of course. Yes! I will marry you."

I take the tab off what's not a shoestring but a drawstring for a pair of sweats and put it in his hand. I grinned, laughter fizzing in my stomach like a shaken pop. "Would you, dear, put the ring on my finger?"

I bat my eyes. Because I'm a woman and I can.

"Um, I'd love to, but I can't."

"Can't? A strong man like you? You have two hands, yes?"

A burly Chicago wind is blowing along the beach.

He matches my smile with one of his own. I'm not going to get the better of him.

"As you wish."

He takes the ring from my hand, kneels (smart man, darn it), and slips the ring tab onto my left hand, locking eyes with me. Then he stands, his hand returns to his waist, and his right pulls me close. He kisses me again.

In his one-armed embrace, I am whole, loved, accepted—and playful.

I take my arm off his back, reach for his hand on his waistband, and move it into a two-armed embrace. We laugh together, as the Chicago wind—and gravity—does its thing.

Who would have expected flannel, heart-print boxers?


The End

# Acknowledgments

To my Lord, Jesus, who told me (through his apostle, Paul) not to conform to the ways of this world, but to be transformed by the renewing of my mind. As usual, You are right.

To my love, Deb, without whom this writing thing would be impossible. Heck, none of "this" (motions widely around himself) would be possible.

Samara is a real place you can visit. And I encourage you to do so. Thank you to Linda Eales, SAMARA Associate Curator, and to the John E. Christian Family Memorial Trust, Inc. http://www.samara-house.org/ Anything I got wrong is my fault, not Linda's.

# About the Author

Michael Ehret has accepted God's invitation to write and is also a freelance editor at WritingOnTheFineLine.com. In addition, he's worked as editor-in-chief of the ACFW Journal magazine for the American Christian Fiction Writers (ACFW), was editor-in-chief of the Christian Writers Guild, and he pays the bills as a marketing communications writer. Michael sharpened his writing and editing skills as a reporter for The Indianapolis News and The Indianapolis Star.

He's been married for 36 years to Deb and they have three children, one dog (a miniature Schnauzer named Baxter), and a granddog. Since he writes fiction by the seat of his pants, who knows what's next? Connect with him at https://writingonthe fineline.com or on Facebook.

# You May Also Like ...

**Other contemporary romance novellas from Scrivenings Press:**

*Much Ado about Romance*

*A novella collection*

**The Marry Wives of Sweetheart by Shannon Sue Dunlap**—Mrs. Augusta Page knows best—for her daughter, Anne, and the whole town of Sweetheart, Texas. When Anne's former boyfriend, Connor Fenton, returns after many years of absence, it's a rocky road to reconciliation. Joshua attempts to rekindle their romance, but Anne's wounded heart never forgave him when he left her behind for the big city.

Augusta enlists the help of her longtime buddy Veronica "Ronnie" Ford to do a little matchmaking, but obstacles abound. Her husband is against the romance, and foolish friend-of-the-family John Falstaff has taken a shine to Anne and asked for assistance. But the biggest obstacle is her daughter's stubborn heart. Mrs. Page and Mrs. Ford have their work cut out to inspire Anne Page to join the ranks of the "marry" wives of Sweetheart.

**The Tempest in the Bay by Susan Page Davis**—A famous writer has retreated to an island home with only his daughter. For ten years, he's hidden away and not sent his publisher any new manuscripts. His daughter Violet is now 20 and wondering if it's time for her to see more of the world since her contact with the mainland is only through Darrell, a rather sluggish man from the shore community who brings out supplies once a month.

Paul's brother Barney and the CEO of his publisher's company set out on a yacht to track him down. But a storm intervenes, and when the sailing party lands on his island, Paul isn't sure he wants to go back.

**Much Ado about Matrimony by Linda Fulkerson**—Tricia Waters has resigned herself to the fact she'll never have a happily ever after, so she focuses on making her cousin's upcoming wedding a memorable one. But when she discovers her ex-fiancé is the best man, she vows to evade him. That is, until the two must work together to prevent the happy couple from breaking up.

Reeling from a personal tragedy, Dr. Ben McIntyre travels to serve as his buddy's best man only to discover the maid of honor is the love of his life. Or she was, until she ended their engagement six years earlier. He plans to keep his distance from Tricia. When circumstances keep pushing them to work together, Ben learns that avoidance is futile.

Get your copy here:

https://scrivenings.link/muchadoaboutromance

*Love Delivered*

*A novella collection*

***Romance at Register Five* (by Amy R Anguish)**—Mack McDonald isn't happy about the Grocerease app coming to his grocery store. But he's committed to the sixty-day trial period, and braces himself to lose money. Kaitlyn Daniels loves how the Grocerease app helps her make ends meet so she can assist her mom, the reason she moved to small Sassafras, AR. Mack and Kaitlyn struggle to overcome differing opinions on the perks of the app. But if they don't, it could keep them from something even better.

***Where Love is Planted* (by Sarah Anne Crouch)**—Ivy Aaronson is surrounded by family at their flower shop in West Texas—just the way she likes it. But she's given up hope on ever finding a man who understands her choices. When attorney Grant Keller orders flowers for his mother, Ivy wonders if maybe there are indeed some considerate men left in the world…until she finds out Grant's relationship with his parents is less than ideal. How can Ivy ever find love when every man she meets puts career over family?

***Sweet Delivery* (by Heather Greer)**—After winning Cake That, Will Forrester thinks his Pastry Perfect Baking Dreams have come true. The sweetness fades when a chain bakery moves to town, and Will must adjust his plans to keep his customers. Hiring Erica Gerard is one of those changes. As they work together, Erica challenges Will and offers new ideas to improve the bakery. Soon, Erica and Will start bringing out the best in each other. But Erica harbors a secret, and if it's discovered, Will might never be the same.

***The Mermaids, the Ex, and USSS* (by Rachel Herod)**—Braig Sanborn is the most loyal employee the United States Shipping Service has ever seen, which is why he agreed to transfer across the country with only a few weeks' notice. Bailey Bivens is so busy planning a friend's wedding, she didn't expect to fall for the carrier who delivers packages to her house. When they both find themselves in too deep, will they agree the relationship was doomed from the start?

Get your copy here:

https://scrivenings.link/lovedelivered

***Love in Any Season***

*A novella collection*

***Spring Has Sprung***—by Regina Rudd Merrick

Laurel Pascal, Assistant City Manager of Spring, Kentucky, is tasked with organizing the town's beloved Daffodil Festival, and she's not happy. An allergy sufferer all her life, she dreads the season from the first Daffodil bloom in the yard to the last coat of pollen on her car. Newcomer Dr. Owen Roswell volunteers to help, and soon finds that not only does Laurel need his expertise as an allergist, but help in appreciating the season she's obligated to celebrate.

What does he want more—for Laurel to fall in love with his favorite season? Or him?

*The Missing Piece*—by Amy R. Anguish

Beth Norton and Tommy England grew up together with best-friend moms who had a love of quilting and a business celebrating the craft. When high school ended, though, so did Beth and Tommy's friendship.

When Tommy moves back after seven years and his mother's death, he can't understand why Beth is so angry with him. Helping Beth and her mother stabilize the finances of the business, they're forced to work together. As Tommy sorts through his mother's things, he finds an unfinished quilt, and it turns into a joint project.

With each stitch taken, they work toward more than just a completed blanket.

*A Sweet Dream Come True*—by Sarah Anne Crouch

Isaac Campbell is living his dream of running an ice cream shop but fears he won't last past the first difficult year. Mel Wilson is a busy single mother who longs to be a chocolatier but is too afraid to turn her dreams into reality.

When Mel and Isaac meet at Bestwood, Tennessee's fall festival, it seems like divine providence. But once Mel agrees to help Isaac bring in customers by selling her chocolates at his shop, she realizes how challenging running a business can be.

Can Mel and Isaac trust in God's provision and make a leap of faith? Will their partnership end in disaster, or will it be a sweet dream come true?

*Sugar and Spice*—by Heather Greer

Emeline Becker, owner of Sugar and Spice Bakery, loves New Kuchenbrünn, except for the gingerbread. As the only bakery, she supplies the annual Gingerbread Festival with the one treat she can't stand. It's gingerbread everywhere.

Things get worse when Ryker Lehmann is hired as the festival photographer. He was her secret teen crush, her sister's boyfriend, and witness to her worst humiliation. Plus, he broke her sister's heart and bruised hers when he left town after graduation. Now, he's back in town, determined to fix their friendship before the festival ends.

With gingerbread and Ryker together, can Emmie make it through the festival with her mind and heart intact?

Get your copy here:

https://scrivenings.link/loveinanyseason

~

*Carolina Connections*

## A Southern Breeze Series: Book Four

Enjoy two novellas connected to Regina Rudd Merrick's A Southern Breeze series in one convenient volume. Both of these stories were included in multi-author collections: "Pawleys Aisle" (Coastal Promises) and "Mr. Sandman" (Candy Cane Wishes and Saltwater Dreams). Now you can complete your collection of A Southern Breeze stories with this novella duo, Carolina Connections.

**Pawleys Aisle**—Leaving a lucrative position in the banking world for the creative world of weddings, Chelsea Prince finds the perfect venue, Pawleys Island Chapel, next door to the perfect walled garden. Her elderly neighbor and partner-in-planning have an agreement, but when the unexpected happens, she has to deal with the cranky grandson who wants to be left alone to write the next great American novel. Since Chelsea has sworn off men, it shouldn't be a problem to ignore him and go on her way hosting weddings in the chapel. But when Marc McCallum offers up a compromise, she wonders if maybe there is one man out there who can be trusted.

**Mr. Sandman**—Events manager Taylor Fordham's happily-ever-after was snatched from her, and she's saying no to romance and Christmas. When she meets two new friends—the cute new chef at Pilot Oaks and a contributor on a sci-fi fan fiction website who enjoys debate—her resolve begins to waver. Just when she thinks she can loosen her grip on thoughts of love, a crisis pulls her back. There's no way she's going to risk her heart again.

https://scrivenings.link/carolinaconnections

www.ingramcontent.com/pod-product-compliance
Lightning Source LLC
Chambersburg PA
CBHW070659100726
47907CB00007B/2268